INFERNO

BENSON FIRST RESPONDERS
BOOK 9

LISA PHILLIPS

TWO DOGS PUBLISHING, LLC.

eBook ISBN: 979-8-88552-251-9

Paperback ISBN: 979-8-88552-252-6

Published by Two Dogs Publishing, LLC. Idaho, USA

Cover Design by Sasha Almazan and Gene Mollica, GS Cover Design Studio, LLC

Edited by Christy Callahan, Professional Publishing Services

Audiobook published by Recorded Books

INFERNO

ONE

Twenty years ago

Conditions were perfect. Tonight was the night.

Richard sat in the front seat of his "nondescript compact." Or so the police had taken to referring to his vehicle on the news. They had yet to get the color right, considering he repainted it every week or so—and switched out the license plates.

No one ever got close enough to see the VIN number.

Or his face.

He watched the building for a while, imagining the way it would look soon enough. His best work could never be rushed. The moment his desire couldn't be swayed by prudence, it was going to prove his downfall. The ability to be patient had been his greatest strength thus far. Every night he waited for the perfect conditions to create his work.

One day he would achieve the ultimate...

The perfect fire.

Tonight had shaped up to be the night. For the past

two weeks, he'd been working on this apartment building. A nudge here. A fix there.

Closing vents.

Sealing sprinkler heads or cutting the wires on the smoke detectors. Disconnecting the fire alarm systems. Finally, he had made sure the basement laundry room would be a tinder box, as it were. Getting in and out quickly, so he wasn't seen or at least remembered much. He used different utility worker uniforms. Gaining access so he could do his work.

His lips curled up just thinking about all that lint buildup.

All that heat with nowhere to go.

As Richard eased out of the car into the muggy air, the door creaked like it always did. He hadn't figured out how to get it to quit yet. Too busy working on his far more important occupation. He knew what the psychologist had said about his obsession, so he had endeavored to suppress the urge.

Until the time was right.

He'd taught himself to control the need to see sweet flames licking up. To feel the heat himself and know that anything burned would be destroyed. He could bring an end to everything, like God himself. It would all burn in the end, all the efforts of man destroyed by fire until nothing remained but what he deemed worthy.

Sweat rolled down the sides of his face as he carried the three shoe boxes down the sidewalk to the building. Downtown, close to the center of Benson. The building was at least forty years old. He had chosen well, not just because of the aging wiring and the lingering heat that made his shirt stick to his skin.

He used a master key copied from the building super

to gain entry to the rear door, down the concrete steps. The one most residents propped open when they ran the dryers—at least in the last week. Inside the laundry room the air hung thick, laced with the scents of detergent and fabric softeners.

Richard set the first device in a dryer, as planned. This one was full of hot clothes because Mrs. Edwin worked the late shift as a nurse and evidently got pulled into overtime tonight. Her son always forgot to retrieve the clothes for her, no matter how many times she asked.

Every component in the shoe box would burn along with everything else.

No evidence.

No way to find him.

He chuckled at the idea of standing in the crowd, watching the building burn like any other spectator.

A shuffle caught his attention. A sniff.

Richard spun around. One of the devices in his hands nearly slid off the other. Almost a disaster, but he caught it and righted the stack in his hands.

He laid them down and went to the source of the disturbance he had heard. Along the row of dryers, then washers. The shelves above were stacked with detergents and empty boxes of dryer sheets. Bundles of lint between them, handfuls tossed up there by the people who actually bothered to clean out lint traps but couldn't seem to find the trash can. That was where he'd had the idea of backing up the vents, blocking all the airflow to trap the fire inside this room.

Wedged between the first washer and the wall, a scraggly dark-haired child wearing threadbare shorts and an oversize T-shirt sat clutching his knees.

Richard crouched. "Are you lost, little boy?"

He shook his head, eyes wide.

"What is your name?"

The kid swallowed. "Custard."

Richard frowned. What a ridiculous name for a child. This building and the people in it all deserved to burn. "Fear not, Custard. It will all be over soon."

But he couldn't have the child be a witness who remembered his face. If he managed to get out.

"You should go back to your apartment. Back to bed." Richard stood. "Now." He said that last word louder than the rest.

At his bark, the child scrambled out and down the hall. A scrabble of feet on the linoleum floor, carrying a teddy bear in one hand. All skinny arms and legs. At least it wouldn't take long for someone his size to fall asleep, minutes before his body was consumed by fire.

Richard yelled after him, "Go!"

He chuckled to himself and set the final ignition devices precisely where he'd planned. Then he used the same door he'd entered, digging the stack of sliced wood from the bush. He wedged one under the door, then two more around the edges—one in the space above the handle and one in the center at the top of the door.

He did the same with the front entrance, ensuring no one inside managed to get out.

And then he sat in his car and waited for the flames.

Thirty minutes later the orange glow of fire lit the night sky. He cracked the window and smelled it on the air, drawing in deep inhales of the rich tang of burning wood.

The smell of cleansing.

Fire truck sirens split the air, coming from the other direction. He never saw them but knew precisely when they pulled up outside the building to find residents banging on the doors. Trapped and trying to get out.

A smile split his lips.

As soon as a crowd gathered, he would join it.

Richard gripped the wheel, eager to go. But he had to be patient.

Red and blue lights flashed in his rearview. He twisted in the seat and found his car suddenly surrounded by a sea of police cars.

Richard gritted his teeth. No. They couldn't have found him! The plan had been flawless! He shoved open the door and stumbled out.

"Richard Sylvana, hands up!"

Cops pointed their weapons at him, positioned behind their cars. Like an invading army in a standoff. "You're under arrest!"

Richard clenched down on his back teeth.

This wasn't over. It would *never* be over.

TWO

Detective Samantha Jesse wasn't on duty for another two hours, which made it the perfect time to be sitting across from her sister in the diner. Not just because Bristol enjoyed the waffles this place served as a special on Fridays, but also because the oven in their apartment was broken again and the company in charge of repairs for the complex hadn't shown up the last three days.

Bristol had nearly white-blond hair, currently braided in what she called her "Viking" braids. Slim figure. Perfect makeup. She kicked Samantha under the table.

Samantha blinked out of her funk about the oven and looked at her sister who lifted her hand and signed, *Pea brain* at her. Bristol motioned to the server standing by their table.

"Huh...what?" Samantha said.

Bristol snorted. She could read lips just fine, and often let out an audible noise like a grunt or groan. She felt laughter in the vibration of the vocal chords in her throat, though a setback in development in the womb had severely impaired her hearing.

Everything else about Samantha's sister was perfect. She was a delicate flower—or so their parents had everyone believe.

Bristol was dynamite wrapped in a delicate exterior. Every guy she met fell head over heels for her, immediately started learning sign language, and inevitably got their heart broken.

Bristol was waiting for "the one."

Samantha told the server, "I'll have the Mediterranean omelet, no sides, and black coffee, please."

Bristol rolled her eyes, understanding perfectly what Samantha had ordered. She lifted the menu and pointed to it.

"The lemon raspberry pancakes?" the server asked. "Syrup?"

Bristol looked at Samantha, who mouthed the word *syrup.* Bristol pointed to something else on the menu.

"Blueberry sauce. Got it." The server took their menus and wandered away.

Bristol signed, *What's on your mind?*

Samantha made a face.

Bristol said, *Tell me.*

Samantha shifted on the bench seat of the booth. Her pistol, tucked in a holster at the small of her back dug into her spine. She might not be on duty, but no way would she remove it and risk leaving it behind. A rookie she'd known years ago did that. He'd been gone from the force two days later.

Bristol signed the letters *C-O-D-A.*

Samantha rolled her eyes. She signed back, *I'm not thinking about him.*

Except that now she *was* thinking about her ex.

At least she didn't have to explain everything to Bristol. Her sister had been there through it all. They'd lived together since Samantha got out of college and Bristol had finished high school. She'd joined the Benson Police Department, where she'd risen up the ranks to Detective First Grade. Intelligence/Major Crimes division. Bristol worked from home as a data entry specialist, but when she wasn't working, she was always out doing something.

Her sister had a vibrant social life with clubs and events all the time for the local deaf community. They had cookouts and went hiking together. This summer a group of them had run a series of 10k races as a team, raising money for services for deaf kids in Benson.

Samantha had lost a partner early this year—yet another guy who'd been half in love with her sister. She'd been transferred to Intelligence, where she was partnered with Jasper Hollingsworth, who had shortly thereafter quit to go work for Vanguard, a private investigations company—thankfully before he could meet Bristol. She liked her current partner, newly minted detective Romeo Alvarez, just fine.

He would not be meeting Bristol, *ever*. Samantha needed him focused on his new detective position.

Still, she was aware her sister thought her life void of any semblance of "fun." Even if they had vastly different definitions of precisely what fun meant.

No way was Samantha running a 10k.

She lifted her right hand and touched her thumb to her breastbone. *I'm fine.*

Bristol rolled her eyes and sat back while the server put their plates down.

Samantha said, "Thanks."

"Anything else I can get you?" The server stepped back and glanced at them both.

Samantha knew her sister's coffee preference well enough to say, "More creamer?"

"Sure thing."

Bristol flipped the little dish upside down on the table and removed it, like a cup and ball magic trick. She took the creamer she'd upended on the table and added more to her coffee—until it was more creamer than coffee. And yet her sister didn't seem to be affected by the high sugar diet she ate.

It was almost enough to convince Samantha to take up running.

Almost.

Samantha ate a couple of bites, then set her fork down. *My new partner is a runner.*

He cute? Bristol's brows rose.

Samantha chuckled. *You're looking for a new guy already?*

Her sister had broken up with a chump a few weeks ago. Samantha had thought they might stay together, but Bristol didn't tell her what the issue was. Just that it was over.

Her sister glanced at the window and watched a couple of cars pass.

The server delivered the creamers. "Anything else?"

Samantha shook her head. When the server turned, she reached across the table and waved at the edge of Bristol's field of vison. After Bristol turned back to her, Samantha motioned at the extra creamers.

The door at the far end opened, and a man stepped in.

Bristol lifted her hands, but Samantha's instincts woke up as soon as she spotted the guy. Her sister knocked her hand on the table, but Samantha signed, *Hold on.*

Samantha watched the man sweep into the room, shove past the hostess, and pull a handgun from under a trench coat.

He swung it around. "No one move!" The guy turned to point the gun at the hostess, who scrambled back, screaming. "Give me all the cash and credit cards in here! This is a robbery."

Samantha edged to the end of the table. She slid her phone across to her sister, unlocking it with her thumb print. She mouthed, *911*, knowing her sister would use text to communicate with emergency dispatch.

"Sir!" She stood, holding both hands up. Needing all his attention on her. "I'm sure the server can get what you want if you give them a second." She kept her tone light.

Beside her, she heard a guy whisper, "Let's tackle him. We'll take him down."

Samantha stopped. "*No one* is going to move. Everyone is going to stay right where they are." With her sister behind her, Bristol likely only had a limited understanding of what was going on. She wouldn't be able to read Sam's lips on anything she said. She might be able to read this gunman's lips, but she'd know enough to ask for police officers.

"That's right!" The gunman waved his weapon around, not pointing it at anyone in particular. "No one moves, just give me the money or I start shooting!"

Samantha couldn't protect everyone in the room from

getting hit. Who knew where he'd be pointing that gun when he squeezed the trigger, either intentionally or accidentally. All she could do was attempt to draw his fire.

With no vest on.

She had her badge—out of sight—and her gun on her, but those would be a last resort. All she had to do was stall him long enough for backup to show and keep any of these people from getting hurt.

The gunman swung his weapon around again, leveling it on a woman between the first row of booths and the kitchen hatch. "You! Get me the money from the register!"

She flinched and dropped a tray. The sound of shattering pottery exploded like a gun going off. Samantha heard her start to cry.

"Someone better *get me my money!*"

The guys in the booth by Samantha were getting antsy. She took a couple of steps toward him to cut them off, and he spotted her coming. Samantha stopped. "What's your name?"

He stared at her.

"I'm Samantha, what's your name?"

"Doesn't matter. I want the money. You gonna get it for me, or am I gonna blow your head off?"

"Killing people won't get you what you want." She took another tiny step, all his attention focused on her. The gun pointed at her. "Tell me your name."

"I.P. Freely."

Samantha didn't react. Across the room a mom and two kids were crying, huddled in the corner, and this guy was making jokes? "Maybe we could sit down, Mr. Freely. Have some breakfast and talk."

"I want money. Don't you know how to listen, woman?"

She didn't want to get into whatever relationship issue put that ire in his voice. "I'm listening. That's my job, to listen to what you want."

"Just give me the *money*, and no one gets hurt."

"No one is going to get hurt," Samantha said. "But in order for me to help you, you'll need to put that gun down."

"I'll kill you and everyone in here!" the gunman shouted.

"Don't make this worse than it is." Samantha had to diffuse this situation. No one from the servers to the manager, if they were even here, had appeared with money to appease the man. If he left, the people inside the diner would be safe and the police could take up the job of finding him.

With Sam on his tail the guy wouldn't get far.

She got her gun out of the holster at the small of her back and lifted it at a forty-five in front of her. Held it in a loose grip. Not aimed at the gunman, but he knew who she was now.

The gunman's expression turned thunderous. They were at the precipice, where they either tumbled down the other side of the steep cliff or she finished this.

"Gun down on the floor," Samantha ordered. "Face the wall, hands behind your head."

His expression contorted into an angry rage.

The door to the diner flung open and two uniformed officers came in, guns out. "Down. Weapon down. On the floor. Nice and easy."

The first officer, an African American woman strode

in, all confidence and that command presence every cop needed.

Her partner followed, an older Caucasian guy with stubble on his cheeks and a smudge of ketchup on his uniform shirt.

Samantha moved to the gunman. She saw that he'd relented in his expression and the sudden slump of his shoulders. She took the gun from his hand and passed it off to the officer, then pulled out her cuffs and secured him.

A smattering of applause sounded around the room. Then someone said, "We need help! He's having a heart attack!"

Sam handed the gunman off to the officers. "Call for an ambulance." She rushed to an older man across the room, clutching his throat. Not his arm. "Can't breathe?"

"He's having a heart attack!" A woman clutched his arm, jostling him. Panicked.

"Let go." She bent and put her head to the man's chest. Heard an erratic heartbeat. The man's panicked gaze met hers, and she saw the fear in his eyes. "Up we go." Samantha grabbed him around the chest, lifting him with her arms under his armpits.

The woman wailed, "What are you doing?"

She got her hands in position and jerked up hard and fast to his diaphragm. The guy coughed and a chunk of some kind of meat flung across the room. He sputtered and gasped. "Thanks."

Sam helped him to a chair just as the EMTs ran in. Thankfully.

Bristol grinned across the room, signing, *Teach me how to do that.*

Samantha rolled her eyes. She went over to her sister,

grabbed her coffee, and sat on the edge of the table, finishing it. She shot her sister a look of exasperation and signed, *Nice breakfast.*

They really needed to get the oven fixed.

A male voice called out, "Jesse!" across the room.

Samantha turned to see her partner ease between two people and move her way through the crowd. Romeo Alvarez stopped by her, took one look at her sister, and sort of froze.

Here we go again.

THREE

Fire Captain Julio Espinoza-Vasquez tipped his coffee cup toward himself and saw just a ring of dry coffee at the bottom of the mug. He straightened it and looked the clock. After six in the evening—just over halfway through his twenty-four-hour shift. It had been a long day.

No way there would be good coffee in the firehouse kitchen this time of evening. He'd have to boil water in the kitchen kettle and make French press in the tiny bunk room he called an office that was only two feet longer than his lieutenant's office.

Down the long conference table in the kitchen, two of the shift firefighters were playing chess. At the other end, an older firefighter who'd been here longer than Julio read a battered sci-fi paperback.

Julio locked the iPad and set it on the table, reaching up with both arms and stretching.

"Hard day?" The old timer didn't even look up from his paperback.

"I was reading the file from that callout last week, the little girl?"

The paperback lowered. "Yeah?" The guy's mustache shifted.

"Arson found the accelerant, but it might be tough to locate the customer who purchased it."

One of the guys playing chess lifted his chin from his hand and glanced over. "Did they tie it to the Wilson Street fire?"

"Not explicitly."

"Because it isn't connected." The guy's brow rose. "Or because no one wants to use the words *serial arsonist*?"

Julio's phone buzzed in his pocket. He ignored it, about to continue the conversation when one of the younger firefighters on shift strode in and said, "Cap, the chief wants to see you."

Julio pushed his chair back and took the iPad with him to set his bowl in the sink. The rookies were on KP duty tonight, and they'd be responsible for all the cleanup in the kitchen after their spaghetti dinner.

He didn't get those duties anymore. He'd been on rotation for bathrooms and the kitchen for years. These days he had to write the schedule and file reports. He also had to call firefighters into his office if they needed to shape up. Or give them praise for a job well done. All part of ranking up in any organization, becoming a manager.

But he still missed the day-to-day of riding truck.

Julio strode right through the open door into Chief Greyson Frayer's office. "Chief." He looked around. "You ever miss cleaning toilets?"

Greyson barked a laugh. The skin on his hands, below the sleeves of his shirt, and above the collar, showed the telltale burns of someone who'd battled a fire. He might've lost a lot—but he hadn't lost everything.

Julio wasn't sure he could continue being a firefighter, even in the chief's chair, after getting burned the way Greyson had. But the guy was a hero, and firefighting was in his blood.

"Can't say I do." Greyson had gray hair on his temples, but the fact he'd fallen in love a few months ago and was about to get married in a matter of weeks meant these days he looked younger than he had in years.

Julio would be surprised if he didn't look ancient. He certainly felt it, settling into the chair across from Greyson's dark wood desk. Used to be the desk didn't have anything on it but work stuff, the photos of his mom and his late father, and pictures of his sister's family were on the shelves in the corner. Now there was a fake plant in the corner of the office, Greyson had a new thermal mug, and the photo facing him that Julio couldn't see was likely a copy of their engagement picture.

"You saw the arson report?"

Julio nodded.

"They officially tied it to the other two fires. Though, you didn't hear that from me. At least, not on the record."

"Got it, Chief."

Greyson wiggled his mouse. "Commander Herrington wants every chief in the city to report in immediately when we come across a fire that might be arson. Especially ones where it appears to have been altered in some way to make the fire more catastrophic."

"So it's for sure, then." Julio shifted on the chair. "Someone is setting fires and making sure there's maximum damage."

"Not only that. They're ensuring that lives are lost."

"I thought there weren't any casualties in the first two fires?"

Greyson winced. "It wasn't released with the rest of the information. Arson Investigation is keeping things close to the vest, but a body was discovered at the second fire. An older woman. They believe the first was a test. His attempt to perfect the scene and get it right. No one died."

"But someone was in the second. It was an abandoned house, right?"

"A foreclosure, that's correct." Greyson nodded. "Until we cleared the scene a couple of days later, we didn't realize there was a body in the basement. Back corner, in a closet."

"Could've been there before the fire."

"Not according to the autopsy," Greyson said. "The victim died in the fire."

Julio blew out a breath. "I wasn't on shift when it happened, but I heard about it after. Still, Arson is keeping all this under a tight lid. Is that a good idea?"

"I know." Greyson nodded. "Secrets don't do anyone any good, especially considering everything that happened with your predecessor."

The captain before Julio had been stripped of his rank and fired for having an affair with a female under his command, and for harassing other female firefighters. He'd also taken a harsher approach with rookies, especially the females.

"The higher the quality of our firefighters," Julio said, "the better the whole department is. But that doesn't mean we degrade them until they meet the standard." He leaned forward on the chair and put his elbows on his knees. "It also doesn't mean we get integrity through transparency by keeping secrets from the public."

"You want a panic in the city?" Greyson paused. "What happened years ago was a mess. Hard to believe the impact is still being felt, but it was a different department back then. We are who we are now."

"We need to trust people. Tell them the truth."

Greyson stared at him. "Commander Herrington advised me to state clearly that if the media obtains any information about these fires, or the person who might be setting them, and the leak is traced back to a firefighter, that person will be fired."

Julio pressed his lips together.

"So how are we going to get the word out without anyone tracing it back to us?"

He blinked. "Um...Chief?"

"We can't keep people in the dark." Greyson leaned forward. "You know that, and I know that. But we need to play this smart. Feed someone enough information the media connects the dots and it can't be traced back to us."

"I'll take another look at the files. See what I can think of."

"Good." Greyson pushed his chair back. "I'm heading out."

"Ashlynn busy tonight?"

The chief's expression softened. "The PD commissioner has an event, and she's on hand for that. Something with Vanguard Investigations, I believe. A fundraiser. I'm headed to my house to finish painting the dining room so I can get ready to sell it." He grabbed a backpack from the floor beside him and stood, setting the bag on the chair.

"Have a good night."

Greyson nodded. "Be safe."

Julio jogged down the stairs and wandered the halls back to the residence half of the firehouse, from the half where two stories of offices housed staff who worked normal nine-to-fives. He preferred to be closer to the engine bay even if he drove a red truck with the department emblem on it, only going to scenes as the commander.

His phone buzzed again, and he tugged it out.

From his mom and dad, in a thread with them both even though his dad didn't text much—the old man preferred the face-to-face of a video call. She'd sent a photo of their latest bowling scores. Julio grinned. She'd improved. He texted back,

> I need to go again soon. See if I can beat your high score.

He added a couple of emojis and sent it. A few seconds later he got a couple back, then a firetruck and a firefighter guy along with the words,

> Be safe.

Overhead, the dispatch alarm sounded. Ringing through the halls. "Truck eight. Ladder seven. Warehouse fire. Multiple victims trapped."

A rush of feet came almost immediately, everyone heading to the engine bays. Julio tugged the turnout pants from the slender closet in his bunk room, then pulled on the same turnout coat he'd worn for years. The name CODA on the back had been a decision the brass made when they discovered the double-barrel last name wasn't going to fit on the jacket. He wasn't going to choose which of his parents to honor, so in his own way he honored them both.

And the nickname stuck, as if it was a regular nickname and not a lot more.

He jogged out the double doors to the empty engine bay, now an expanse of gleaming floor and rows of shoes on either side of where the trucks would've been parked. A swivel chair in the corner, close to the pool table, still rotated.

He strode to his captain truck. The drive to the scene in the wake of two speeding red trucks with lights and sirens going was quick, and he pulled up down the street. The trucks had offloaded personnel and were already rolling out hoses to spray down the flames lighting up the building from inside. Black smoke poured out into the sky.

This end of town, the business was manufacturing, but he had to get on the phone with dispatch to find out who leased the unit. With his clipboard and pen, and the information scribbled in the corner, Julio slapped on his helmet and went to the center of the chaos.

He dialed up his radio and listened to the back and forth between his lieutenants and their people. In a brief break in the conversation, he said, "This is Captain Coda. Situation report."

The ladder lieutenant stood at the bottom of the unit on top of his truck. He grasped the radio on his jacket and replied, "Two pairs on a search of the east side, two outside ascending to the second floor now. We've got people trapped on this side of the building."

They must've seen them in the window and decided to get up there from the outside. Meanwhile, their colleagues did a room by room search of the same part of the building from the inside.

Julio wanted to say a prayer for them, but the most feeling he nursed for God these days was a whole lot of anger. *The Lord giveth and the Lord taketh away* was certainly true. But he couldn't finish the expression. Not with the way he raged inside.

"Copy that," Julio said. "Truck report."

Static crackle greeted him.

Julio scanned the building. Flames licked out of broken windows up into the evening sky. Not yet dark, he could see the color of the smoke. "Not good." He lifted his radio. "All positions, evac now. I repeat, evac now. This thing is turning deadly."

Two firefighters fled out the front doors, followed by a third.

"Out!" Julio yelled into the radio. "Everyone out!"

The ladder guys paused. Someone screamed from inside the window.

A second later an explosion from deep inside the building rocked the structure.

And then it started to collapse in on itself.

FOUR

Samantha led the way out of the residential house and back to the car, parked at the curb. Her department vehicle was an old dark-red Toyota with a hundred fifty thousand miles on it, and temperature controls that only worked when they chose to.

She beeped the locks and opened the driver's door.

On the other side of the car, Romeo pulled open his door. "So that was a bust."

She tipped her head to the side in a kind of nod and slid in. "Her dad, I'm guessing. He convinced her not to say anything."

"So the kid gets away with harassing her?"

Samantha pulled the car away from the curb. "Nothing we can do with no testimony and no physical evidence."

It would be a measure of the kind of cop he was, what Romeo did when his hands were tied in an investigation. How they reacted said a lot about a person's character when they had no power in a situation.

As for her, she gripped the wheel. Maybe just more

used to it? Feeling powerless never sat right. Who on earth would say that they were fine with it? She just had more experience—not just in her years on the job. She knew what it felt like to have no control.

Or no voice, the way so many assumed of her sister.

Plenty of people had dismissed Bristol as having no feelings, or no will, just because she had no way to communicate with a hearing person who didn't know her language. Just because she couldn't understand what a person said out loud didn't mean she had nothing to say. That wasn't all communication could be—or should be.

Life was about adapting to the situation you were in.

Making the best of it.

Romeo tapped his phone on his leg. "I'll text my sister. She's SRO at the East Benson High School. Maybe she knows this kid and she can keep an eye on him."

Samantha nodded.

"And in the meantime, you can tell me who your friend was."

She smiled but didn't open her lips. Of course, he asked again. He'd been asking all day. Almost as if he'd fallen in love at first sight this morning at the diner—with her sister.

"She's who you were having breakfast with, right?"

"Correct." And they didn't look alike enough that he'd immediately pegged them as siblings. Bristol looked like their mother, while Samantha took after their father.

"You can't even tell me her name?"

Samantha figured her sister had already looked Romeo up online if he had profiles. A lot of cops didn't keep social media except anonymous accounts for work. Bristol probably knew everything about him.

"You're a detective." Samantha shrugged one shoulder. "Detect."

Romeo shifted in his seat. "This is a test of the rookie. A hazing thing."

"If it helps you sleep at night."

"Do you do this to all your partners?" he asked.

"To be fair, I'm usually the rookie," she replied. "Guess you drew the short straw getting me as your training partner."

"Or they're easing me in gently."

She laughed. "Right. That's a cop thing to do, for sure."

"Good point. My first training officer out of the academy didn't let me drive for six months."

She pulled up at a stoplight and looked over. "I probably won't make you wait *that* long."

"I appreciate it."

She looked to the front again, a smile stretching her lips wide.

"What about for old times' sake?" he pressed. "Is that enough for you to tell me who she is?"

"You're really gonna pull the 'we got blown up together' card?"

"Will it work?"

She chuckled, trying to decide if she was hungry enough for food or if they should just hit a gas station and get a soda. "You don't even remember it. You were in critical condition, and I hit my head. We didn't go through a foxhole moment together."

"Shame."

"How have we never talked about what you do remember?"

He fiddled with the radio dials but didn't change

anything. "I get flashes of entering the house sometimes. I know it had to do with the case Stella and Eric were working, those domestic terror guys in the woods who turned out to be his family. I remember every moment of recovery. Every inch I had to push to get back what the injury was trying to take from me."

"I remember waking up after." Throwing up. A screaming headache.

The rest of it...those things she tried not to think about. Ever.

That day was a dividing line in her life between who she had been before and who she was now. The life she would've lived if the day had gone differently. Her life as it was, and now. This.

Her phone buzzed and lit up in the bracket on her dash, to the left of the steering wheel. "What's that about?"

He looked at his own cell. "Callout from dispatch. All available units. It's a couple blocks from here. There's a fire, and the department has firefighters trapped. They need crowd control."

She grabbed the radio out of the cupholder and handed it to him. "Call us in as responding." Samantha flipped the lights and sirens on and waited for traffic to slow. She flipped a U-turn in the middle of the street and tapped her phone until it showed her directions to the address.

Then she hit the gas.

"Crowd control?"

Yeah, not their usual thing.

But that area? If he was on shift, he would be there.

"There's a firefighter..." How was she supposed to explain it? "I know him." She gripped the wheel, flying through intersections. Just a few miles away. Was he all right? It was enough to convince her to pray. He believed. She believed. It was just that the knowledge never did her any good.

It never made her life better.

Faith didn't change the fact that anytime she had something good, it was taken away.

Gone.

"Overtime money, and more time to convince you to give me her number?" Romeo paused. "We can check on your friend."

Samantha didn't respond to that. Right now she had to keep things tight, get herself in check. Going this fast she had to be far more careful than usual, or a quick trip could turn deadly before they even got to the scene.

A trickle of smoke scented air floated into the interior of the car.

When she turned the corner onto the street where the industrial district was packed together, the yellow glow of flames came into view.

The building had toppled in on itself.

"That's bad," Romeo said. "We need to get these people back. They might be looking to help, but they don't have gear."

Two more fire trucks turned the corner behind them. Samantha got out of the way and decided to just park here. They pulled on PD windbreakers and headed over. Romeo had the radio, and she pocketed her cell phone. Badge on her belt. Gun on her hip. As if any of it would protect her from flames.

That was his job.

Was he even here?

"Looking for your friend?"

She glanced at Romeo, walking beside her down the waterlogged sidewalk. They stepped over a fire department hose and came up to a crowd of about eight people. Two cops. "All right, everyone!" Samantha called out. "Back up, and keep going. We need to clear this area!"

Romeo started ushering people back.

"Sergeant!" She got the attention of the cop who ranked highest, at least so far. "Where do you want us?"

"We'll get a barricade up. If you find anyone on this side of it, send them my way."

"Copy that, Sarge." She didn't know him, just the uniform and the chevrons on his sleeves. But the fact she'd been ordered to have free reign of this side of the divider between civilians and first responders meant she could look for Julio.

There.

She spotted his truck, the commander on scene vehicle he drove. Captain over the trucks that had responded and the personnel who worked on them.

"Where are you, Julio?"

Never mind that she had no right to care. No right to walk in and demand an update from a bunch of firefighters she'd either never met or hadn't spoken to in years.

Samantha walked around, looking for the fire department on scene commander. They were all working the scene—like these two disheveled firefighters pulling an older man from the rubble.

Someone yelled, "Get me airbags! We need to get this wall stabilized." But it wasn't him. It was a lieutenant.

She shouldn't disturb them. There was more at stake here than her care for one man. Surely, he was all right.

You wouldn't be that cruel, would You?

Months ago, she'd been trapped in a house. Julio had responded with firefighters and helped get her out.

She hadn't seen him since.

Her stomach roiled. She checked her phone and decided to search for opportunistic civilians on her way to reconvene with her partner.

Romeo stood by the crowd, talking to a couple, and another man. As she approached, she heard him say, "...let the first responders do their jobs."

She stood beside him. "It's pretty chaotic over there. If we steer clear, they'll be able to focus."

Romeo nodded.

The couple turned away. Down the street, a news van pulled up.

"Great," she muttered.

Romeo hissed a breath. "Of course, it's my ex."

Samantha looked at him. "Maxine Careu is your ex?"

"Not my finest moment." Even in the darker evening light, his cheeks flushed. "I broke it off a few months ago, and she doesn't seem to have got the message."

As far as Samantha was concerned, that was even more reason not to give him her sister's number. Bristol didn't need to get to know a guy who went through women the way most people went through a loaf of bread. They probably wouldn't even be able to have a basic conversation.

"Romeo!" Maxine waved, trotting over on ridiculous heels.

One of the people beside Samantha snorted.

Behind Maxine, a burly guy carried a camera over his shoulder. Maxine stopped in front of them and smoothed down her hair. She batted her eyelashes at Romeo, probably determined to let him know exactly what he was missing. "Can you tell us what's happening here?"

Romeo motioned to the building on fire. "Pretty sure it's exactly what it looks like." There was a definite undercurrent of *unlike you* going on in his tone. "Stay back and let the firefighters do their jobs."

Maxine blinked, evidently surprised to be rejected so cleanly. She glanced at Samantha, and her eyes lit. "Start rolling." She waved her cameraman over.

He lifted the camera, a white light on the front.

"Aren't you the officer who just this morning foiled an armed robbery and saved a man from having a heart attack?"

It's my job.

She could hear the Intelligence sergeant reading her the riot act for saying that already, and she hadn't even spoken aloud. "Please remain behind the barricade, ma'am."

More fire trucks pulled in, and a chief's SUV. She'd met Greyson briefly, enough to know he was a good guy.

Her stomach knotted with worry for Julio. Strong enough she didn't realize she'd gone up to their huddle until she stood right beside the pocket of firefighters. The ones who'd just arrived and three others, covered in soot and ash, and sweat.

One said, "It's primed for a secondary collapse, and there won't be anything we can do about it."

"I want a head count." Greyson, the fire chief at Julio's house, ran a hand down his face. "I want to know who is unaccounted for." He looked around, spotted her but didn't get distracted by the fact she was listening. "Where is the captain?"

"Coda went inside," the firefighter reported. "Right

after the collapse. He pulled us out and then went back in. We haven't heard from him."

"Get to work."

They all disbursed, and Greyson fished out his radio. "This is Chief Frayer. I am in command of this scene. If you are within reach of a radio and able to use it, call out. We will find you." Then he turned to Samantha. "Wanna help?"

"What do you want me to do?"

FIVE

Julio inhaled, the air a mix of dust and ash. He coughed it out, feeling the burn in his throat and lungs. They weren't going to last much longer down here.

"We aren't going to last much longer down here."

He grinned at the kid who'd said that, a rookie firefighter. Martin. The same guy who'd told him Greyson wanted to see him earlier. Now the guy had blood running down his face and a likely-broken ankle. Julio had found him struggling to help out the other guy, currently across from them, toward the front door.

A rumble had sent them tumbling down.

"Don't think there's anything funny about this," the guy across from them said.

"Sorry." Julio wanted to shift his seat but didn't dare move. "I was just thinking the same thing right when he said it."

Julio palmed his flashlight and flicked it on, trying to conserve the battery. No one wanted to sit trapped in near darkness beneath a fire for too long. Even he was starting to dislike it enough he was antsy. "We need a way out of here."

"You heard the chief, Cap. They'll find us."

He was glad the rookie had that kind of faith in his colleagues. Except they had no way to tell anyone where they were. As soon as the call came over the radio, it started to crackle. Then it died before he could respond. Their phones had no signal.

The room around them creaked.

Julio looked at the debris over them. Then he eased away from the wall and got on his knees.

"What are you doing, Cap?"

"We can't push on the ceiling pieces above us," Julio said. "That will dislodge everything down on top of us."

"Great," the muttered voice came from behind him. "Better to put us out of our misery."

He turned to the civilian. "Why don't you tell me what your name is?"

The guy was certainly having a bad day at work, but they needed hope right now. Not the kind of pessimism that meant a slow death to their strength of will. Their need to live through this would help them survive rather than succumb to what he considered inevitable.

He scrunched up his nose. "It's Paul."

Julio said, "We aren't going to die down here, Paul."

The guy made a face but said nothing. He had blood in his hair, the wound back behind his ear. Dislocated shoulder, though he hadn't let Julio take a look at it. He just held the arm close to his front and said, "Worst shift ever." And things like, "This job was never worth it."

"What's behind this?" Julio went to the side, where

he could see concrete that angled up. He'd made sure no one was under it, but could they get above it? The whole thing was a hazard if it came down. Still, there was a chance that if it held, they could use the obstruction to get higher.

Up to where the flames were.

"Maybe stairs," Paul said. "We're on the west side of the building."

Julio shifted a piece of debris. To his right, something creaked and groaned. *I don't want to wait around to die.* He would much rather go out trying to get free.

Water sloshed under his feet.

Exposed pipes in the wall, who knew what they were for. Maybe carbon monoxide pumping into the room to silently kill them.

Yeah, Paul was probably rubbing off on him.

He didn't want to consider this to have been intentional. No one wanted that, even if an accident was senseless and there was often no justice for lives lost. Just because there was a fire didn't mean there was someone to blame for it. Fingers got pointed anyway, whether anyone investigated the origin or not.

People believed whatever they wanted.

Martin moved into the spot beside him. "I'll help." He grabbed a bigger piece of drywall and started to pull it back. "You think we can get out this way?"

"Better than the alternative. At least create an opening so they can hear us call out."

The rookie nodded. "Nearly got it." He shifted the piece a little more, standing with one boot lifted off the floor. The entire room groaned as the pieces around them shuddered and smoke filtered in through the opening,

Julio coughed, more a reflex than anything else, as hot wisps of air made his throat want to close.

He was going to get these guys out. *Right, God?* But he had no standing to ask for help. He'd spent the last two years angry and determined to ignore the fact God even existed. How was he supposed to beg when he had no right?

It would be far easier if he could dismiss the whole thing. Pretend God didn't exist, or even convince himself of it. But he couldn't. He knew the truth too intimately to ever believe otherwise.

So they were at an impasse.

"It's gonna come down!" Paul put his good arm over his head.

"Anyone down there?" The call came from high above Julio, through the opening they'd made.

"We're here!" Martin said. "Burks, Coda, and one civilian!"

"On our way!"

Julio let out a breath. "Let's go, Paul. Time to leave, unless you wanna stay." He went over and got his arm around Paul's middle, on his good side. "Up we go."

Over at the opening, Martin eased out. "Down here." He hopped a couple of steps.

The room shuddered.

Paul whimpered, but Julio just moved him to the gap and said, "Squeeze through."

Firefighters in full gear waited on the other side. Helmets and air tanks—which Julio had slid off when they fell. They grabbed Martin and passed him off up the stairs.

"Gotta move fast," his lieutenant said. "It's pretty unstable."

Julio tried to talk, but no sound came out. He just nodded.

"We were pulling out two others when we heard you. So you can thank the Lord Almighty we did."

Julio handed off Paul to another guy, and the lieutenant said, "Need my air?"

All he could do was shake his head, his throat raw and nearly shut. His head swam. The guy grabbed him around the waist. Julio didn't do much to get himself out, and he was going to get this guy a gift card to his favorite burger place when they were out of here. The lieutenant took his weight and walked him out, lowering Julio to the ground outside.

He blinked. Red and blue flashing lights. There was something immensely comforting to him seeing firefighters move around, and listening to the sound of water spraying on a fire.

"Here." She crouched beside him and held out a water bottle.

Samantha. He stared at her.

"Drink."

Julio took two sips, then poured the rest on his head. The water practically sizzled against the heat of his skin.

"I'm getting an EMT. You don't look good." She started to straighten out of her crouch. Blonde hair longer than the last time he'd seen it, curled down around her shoulders.

He reached up and snagged her hand. Still had his gloves on. Julio left a dark streak on her skin he didn't like.

"What?"

He tried to speak. No words came out.

So frustrating. There were plenty of things he wanted

to say to her, but their personal stuff aside, he also wanted an update on what was going on. At least his brain was getting oxygen, or he'd have a problem right now.

Namely, he'd be passed out and headed for the hospital.

No doubt he was going there anyway, but that wasn't the point right now.

Greyson came over, standing a couple feet back from Julio's boots. "How are you doin'?"

Uh-oh. Julio didn't like that expression. He was going to be in trouble for going in, leaving his command post and pitching in when his guys—and innocent victims— were in trouble. As soon as Greyson knew everyone was all right, reports would be filed.

Julio would get written up. Maybe even suspended.

He tried to say, *Is everyone out?* No sound out of his throat. He lifted his hand and bit down on the edge of his glove, tugging it off.

"He hasn't said anything," Samantha replied for him.

A couple other guys crowded around.

Julio got the other glove off and lifted his hands. He signed to Samantha, *Is everyone out?*

"What's he saying?" Greyson asked her.

His mind slipped back to the times, so many times, he'd interpreted for his parents. Every school activity, doctor appointment, every dinner at a restaurant. Everything. Everywhere. He'd been their connection to the hearing world.

She relayed what he'd said, and the chief turned to the firefighters nearby. "Who is still unaccounted for?"

"No one, now Coda is out." The firefighter motioned to him, then said, "You know sign language?"

Samantha frowned. "What do you think CODA means?"

The guy just shrugged.

"Child of a deaf adult." Samantha folded her arms. "His parents are both deaf."

Julio needed to get them back on track. *Samantha*—he used his sign for her. Their sign. *What caused the building collapse?*

That doesn't matter right now, she signed back. "He needs to go to the hospital."

"That's what he's saying?" Greyson asked.

Julio shook his head. *Do any of the employees know what happened?*

Samantha sighed. "He wants to know what caused this."

Julio looked around just in case there was someone nearby who had created this devastation. Arsonists often hung at the scene and watched the response unfold. A person who did that was sick in the head as far as he was concerned.

But was the concept just fresh in his mind, or was this just a tragedy?

Was this an accident? He patted her leg. *Sam.*

Greyson said, "Why don't you worry about you and I'll worry about the scene, yeah?" The chief walked away.

Julio signed, *I'm in trouble.*

"You think?" Samantha put her hand on her hip. "The EMTs are busy with the other victims."

He wasn't a victim.

Julio tried to talk. All that came out was air, and he dissolved into a coughing fit.

"We need to get you looked at." She glanced around,

spotted the person she was looking for and yelled, "Romeo! Get the car!"

Julio frowned. He spotted Romeo Alvarez, a cop he knew and respected. A guy he'd have said was pretty close to being a friend. But Julio knew exactly the kind of guy he was. Cop or not, he always had a girlfriend. Always looking for something, and he never seemed to find it.

The guy jogged away, keys in one hand.

Julio had found what every man was looking for in eighth grade, when he'd spotted three bullies pushing around a sixth grade girl whose family had just moved to Benson. All arms and legs, and blonde braids. They'd tugged on her hair, hassling her while she could only make noises in response. He'd pegged her as deaf right away.

A second before he shoved the first guy, this older girl his age had stormed over and knocked two kids together. Wading in to fight on her sister's behalf.

He'd been suspended for what he did, but it had been worth it. Those guys backed off hassling Sam's little sister, and he and Samantha were inseparable for the next ten years.

She was with Romeo?

Together?

Julio held out his hand, and the firefighter closest to him hauled him up. He swayed, but there was no way he'd do this not on his own two feet.

She turned to him. "You look terrible, but you'll be the doctor's problem."

While chaos swirled around them he signed, *Romeo?* letter by letter. Then, *Really?* Samantha's expression shifted, and he saw exasperation plain as day.

She said, "You have no idea what—"

He cut her off, dragging her up against him. Julio saw the surprise—but also not—on her face. She knew what he was doing, and why. Because she knew him better than anyone else. The way he knew her...even if it had been two years.

He saw it all there in her eyes.

A second before he touched his lips to hers.

/ SIX

Samantha squeezed the bridge of her nose. Still able to feel his smoky clothes up against her. She didn't want to think about the rest of him, especially when the lines between "supposed to" and "off limits" tended to blur when they were around each other.

"Are you gonna tell me what that was?" Romeo asked.

She looked up, perched on the edge of a chair in the waiting area while Romeo went for a cup of coffee. "Thanks."

He settled beside her and sipped.

She tasted hers—awful, but strong enough to wake her up.

"Nothing? We're just gonna ignore the fact a fire captain grabbed you and kissed you like that in front of everyone. He can't even talk because he ate so much smoke, but everyone heard that statement loud and clear."

Across the other end of the waiting room, two firefighters looked over. They probably heard everything Romeo had just said.

Samantha wanted to crawl under the chair and... never come out. "Finish your coffee and let's go."

She didn't allow hot drinks in the car that didn't have secure lids after her training officer had drilled into her the importance of not having injury hazards. A hot drink in a high-speed chase? No, she'd rather drink fast and then go rather than wind up with a burn on her leg after it spilled.

"We *are* going to talk about this." He leaned slightly toward her. "And that woman."

"She's off limits."

"Really? I hadn't noticed."

Samantha shoved his shoulder, then got up and went over to the firefighters sitting across from them. "How is your guy?"

The older one with the mustache said, "The kid has a sprained ankle. Coda has inhalation. He should be all right, though."

His buddy sitting beside him struggled to keep a straight face. "Heard you gave him mouth-to-mouth."

He was newer and hadn't been on shift when Julio was during the time they'd been together. The older guy had. He knew they'd had an ugly, public breakup two years ago.

"I'm glad it's only minor." She nodded. "Anyone else?"

The older guy said, "Two vics in critical, and the guy Coda got out has a dislocated shoulder. We'll update the PD if you want? After we make sure our boys get back to the station."

She held out her hand, and they shook. "I'd appreciate it."

"You call his next of kin?"

"I checked the paperwork when they admitted him. He still has me listed."

The older guy nodded.

"But I'll make sure his parents know."

"Thanks."

Samantha trailed away to where Romeo stood at the opening into the waiting area.

"You know all the firefighters?" he said. "You know what they do when they're in crisis. How to talk to them."

"And?"

"Just interesting. Like you and Julio using sign language." He stared at her, like trying to figure out a puzzle. "Seems like there's a whole lot about you that I don't know."

"I prefer to keep my personal life personal."

"No kidding." Romeo walked beside her down the hall to the emergency department. "I had figured that out. I'm a detective, you know."

Samantha rolled her eyes.

"But you and I are special. We went through a trauma together, and it bonded us." He laid a hand over his heart. "We're connected."

It didn't surprise her that Julio had done what he did. Even if in the heat of the moment he had the completely wrong idea about who she and Romeo were to each other. So wrong he'd felt the need to make a very loud statement to anyone watching about who belonged to who.

She never had been able to argue with him about what really mattered.

Truth was, deep down she knew it. Like all the way to her soul. She belonged to Julio Espinoza-Vasquez, and she always would. No matter how far apart they were, or if they went years without speaking.

She would always be his.

That kiss hadn't been about what Romeo called their *special bond.* "You and I were at the same scene. The house blew up."

"Exactly. We're connected."

Samantha almost laughed. "That isn't why he kissed me."

"No? He was staking his claim, right?" Romeo blew out a breath. "Fine. Does he know that's not what we are?"

"Doesn't matter. But yes." Just for reasons Romeo would never know. "You were in critical condition. How can we be connected if you weren't even awake?"

Actually, she wasn't sure she wanted to know, so she waved him off.

He slung an arm around her and gave her a squeeze. "Feel better?"

"You're annoying." Of course. He had a sister, and she realized far too late that this must be how Romeo drew his sibling out of a funk if she was ever in one. "But thanks."

"You're welcome."

The sliding doors swept open, and they went outside. The fire chief's car occupied the closest first responder spot. Chief Frayer and another man, an older guy in firefighter officer uniform, headed toward them.

As much as she didn't even want to think about it, Julio had definitely made a *statement.* In front of everyone he worked with, the reporter lady and her camera guy, and all the bystanders. Before too long, everyone in the close-knit first responder community would be contacting her asking for the scoop on her relationship with the quiet fire captain who worked bomb squad.

Which was precisely the reason she'd kept it quiet before, and never talked about it much now.

Chief Frayer said, "I was hoping you were still here."

Why was that? "Coda should be released tonight," Samantha said. "The other guy is getting his ankle looked at. There aren't any serious injuries among the firefighters."

The white-shirt guy said, "That's good."

"Except for the victims in critical condition."

It might've been overshadowed by "the kiss"—as she'd decided to think about it—but Julio had been worried the fire was set on purpose. He'd been insistent that Greyson answer the questions he'd been asking while not even able to talk.

She wanted to speak with Julio about it, but if there was something going on—like an arsonist in Benson—she didn't have the jurisdiction to investigate.

"Is it okay if I email over a file?" Greyson pulled out his phone. "We had a fire two weeks ago. There was a body found in the basement, during cleanup. We believe the victim was killed on purpose during the burn."

"And you need my help? Or the assistance of BPD?" She needed to clarify the request, or she wouldn't know what the expectations were.

"Yours, maybe the whole BPD." Greyson glanced at his colleague. "If you can ID the deceased, it would be a great help toward figuring out who is setting fires."

Samantha caught the seriousness in his tone and nodded. "Of course, I'll take a look."

After she ran it by her sergeant and got the official

sign-off, she would be all over helping to protect firefight-ers. There was only so much they were equipped to protect themselves against, but being a firefighter was arguably more dangerous than being a cop.

Not that she'd tell that fact to any cop she knew.

"We appreciate it." The white shirt seemed to have to force the words out.

Chief Frayer said, "So far there have been two fires. Tonight might be the third. With one deceased, we're looking at patterns. No one wants another death on our hands."

Romeo shifted, his stance what she'd come to recognize as his cop mode. "Where were the other two fires?"

"Both were residences."

"So tonight would be a break in pattern."

The white shirt said, "Or an escalation."

"Captain Tennet works in Arson Investigation." Chief Frayer motioned to the white-shirted older man beside him.

Samantha figured a guy with a little seniority in years might resent someone like Julio who had risen in the ranks quickly. Especially when he was the one the guys on trucks rallied around. They respected their captain—or so she assumed. Back when she and Julio had been together, they'd loved him as their lieutenant.

She wondered if their breakup had to do with the reason he'd focused so heavily on his career. It certainly was why she'd become a detective and worked her way to major crimes.

Though, calling it a breakup didn't quite fit the immensity of what had happened.

Felt more like a giant fissure had spread open between them, sweeping them apart so hard and so fast she hadn't been able to reach out. Let alone grab his hand and allow Julio to tuck her against him. The way he'd done at the scene just a short while ago.

Claiming her in front of her new partner.

What on earth had possessed him to do that?

She couldn't even imagine what he was thinking. And right now talking it over would be far too volatile. She needed space to process it all. About five years would probably suffice.

"Is it okay if we go back to the scene tonight?" she asked, snapping back to reality. "Take a look around?"

Chief Frayer lifted his chin. "If your sergeant signs off on it, let's meet there tomorrow. The fire should've cooled by then enough for us to walk through and assess the damage. Does that sound okay?"

She glanced at Romeo, trying to get a read on what he thought about it. He nodded, so she said, "Sounds good."

Romeo turned to Frayer. "Are you assuming you're likely to find another body in this warehouse, if it was the same guy?"

"I sincerely hope not." The fire chief nodded. "Thank you both for your time."

Samantha told them both bye, and she and Romeo headed for their car. It would smell like smoke—and Julio. That was the last thing she needed when her life was a carefully constructed attempt to not be reminded of him...

And everything she'd lost.

"It doesn't exactly fit a pattern."

She glanced at Romeo over the hood of the car, the moon low in the sky behind him. "And you're an expert at arson investigation now?"

"I might be by morning."

"Thought you were busy trying to find out who my breakfast companion was."

"You're gonna kick a heartbroken man when he's down?" Romeo clutched his chest. "I need something to do to keep my mind from wandering to the most beautiful woman I've ever seen." He paused. "Hey, did she say anything about me after the diner? Did she ask who I was?"

Samantha got in the car, shaking her head. When Romeo slid into the passenger seat, she told him, "If you quit asking about her, I'll let you drive."

He made a stabbing motion into his heart with an imaginary knife. "You know how to wound a man. Maybe I know how Julio feels more than I realized."

Samantha jerked around and pinned him with a stare. "Don't."

Tears burned in the back of her eyes.

"Whoa, Sam. I didn't know." He reached out but didn't touch her. "Sorry. I don't know what I'm talking about."

"And you feel like you're stepping in a minefield."

"Yeah, actually."

"Then stay out of the field," she warned. "That way you don't have to worry about where to step."

She headed for the station so they could clock out and get home. Today had spiraled in a way neither of them expected, but that was the nature of the job.

"We have plenty of other cases," she added. "Maybe tomorrow we…"

"See other people?" Romeo shifted in his seat, glancing in the side mirror. "We're partners. Sorry to break it to you, but you're stuck with me. And apparently the guy who is following us. He doesn't know three's a crowd."

Samantha gripped the wheel. "There's traffic out here. No one is following us."

Still, she drove in circles just to be sure. Looped the block a couple of times. Past the Walmart, and by the library back to the police station downtown—their hub.

But didn't see anyone tailing them.

SEVEN

Julio sipped on the tea he was going to tell *no one* he had in his coffee cup. It tasted slightly of coffee, the way hotel coffeemakers did when someone tried to simply heat water in them. So he was probably getting some coffee molecules. The tea was one his mom had told him would ease his throat.

He'd spent an hour on his day off on video chat with them, while they sat on a bench in the park at the retirement community where they lived in Florida. A place that had full services for deaf residents.

The front doors slid open, and he ducked into the foyer of the Benson Fire Department's main office, two buildings down from the brick building that housed the PD headquarters with the feds squatting in their lobby. This place was newer and had a lot more cool features. The police department had some kind of old-world flare—now it just looked old.

Julio signed in at reception, went through the scanner, and headed up to the conference room where the meeting would start in a few minutes. Sure, he wasn't technically supposed to be back on shift until tomorrow. But what harm would there be in getting information? Listening. Finding out what the latest was on the warehouse fire.

It definitely beat sitting at home in his empty house, trying not to think about Samantha.

Not just because the house was supposed to be *theirs* and she'd never even lived in it.

Julio stepped out of the elevator, spotted the department's lead arson investigator, and lifted his chin. "Dominic."

Captain Tennet lifted his chin back at Julio. "Meeting is about to start."

The older man looked tired, with dark circles under his eyes and the lines on his face more pronounced than usual. He should have shifted to more of a desk job years ago, but who would give up field work if they didn't have to? Julio didn't plan to quit going out on calls anytime soon. Even if he got reprimanded for entering the building.

As if he'd leave his men without someone to aid them getting out.

The fact he'd wound up one of the victims but saved the life of an employee—a civilian—managed to cancel each other out, thankfully.

Maybe Tennet would let Julio help with the case.

At least, that was what he was going to try to get out of this briefing.

He stepped in and saw that half the chairs had been stacked against the wall. Four long rectangular tables had been arranged facing each other, a line of chairs around them. He chose the east side, preferring a corner close to the coffee pot. He could smell it. When he was done with this tea, he needed at least three cups of coffee.

Then he'd feel like he could get going with his day.

Samantha turned from the coffee pot, a paper cup in her hand. Stirring it with a little wooden stirrer which was cuter than it should be. One sugar, no milk or cream.

Did she still remember how he took his?

She spotted him, and the rhythm of her stirring hiccupped. He watched her survey him, assessing his condition? Taking stock of how he looked two days after he nearly died, trapped in that room. After he couldn't talk and they had to sign to each other.

After he kissed her.

No matter that no one had answered his questions. The guys on his truck hadn't quit texting him since, asking about his parents being deaf. Checking he was all right. Asking about the kiss—at least those who didn't know he had dated Samantha, or that they'd broken up two years ago.

Work was way better than sitting at home.

Or trying to burn some energy when he had little to spare to start with. He felt like he needed a nap, which was seriously unhelpful.

She signed, *How are you?* As if she didn't know the answer.

He signed back, *How are* you? Emphasizing *you* like he was issuing a challenge. She wanted to talk to him? That was going to go both ways.

"Hey." Romeo Alvarez slapped Julio on the back, jostling him. "How's it going?"

It *had* been going okay. Now, not so much.

Julio just lifted his chin and took a seat.

Romeo went around the table and sat on the side where Samantha had her stuff out. But she'd done that thing where she put her backpack on the chair beside her, so they weren't right next to each other.

He liked Romeo just fine. The guy was a good guy, a solid believer and a cop, but his history with women? It wasn't that Julio didn't trust him to do the right thing. It was that he didn't trust anyone to treat Samantha right. He wondered if that meant they were destined to be alone forever. Was he resigning her to singleness for the rest of her life just because things hadn't worked out for them?

It wasn't like there had ever been anyone else for him.

Mostly they were at an impasse as far as he was concerned.

Tennet sat down from him, flipping open a paper file. Greyson and a few others had arrived, personnel from the fire department mostly. So why were Samantha and her partner here? Did it have something to do with why they'd been at the scene the other night?

"Okay, let's get started," Greyson said, still standing at one end of the table. "For the sake of those of us who need to be brought up to speed, I'll reiterate the basics. So far we have confirmed three fires are the work of a single assailant, an arsonist. At the second fire, which took place at a residence, a body was discovered shut up in a basement closet."

A woman to Julio's right shuddered. He was pretty sure she did admin for the arson department but hadn't met her before.

Greyson said, "Detective Jesse?"

Samantha nodded. "The woman has been identified as Eva Bronswich, eighty-four years old. A lifetime resident of Benson. No living relatives listed. We're digging more into her life, but it appears she was renting the house where she died."

Romeo leaned back in his chair. "Neighbors said she was quiet, never really had visitors. They hadn't seen her for a few days before her house caught on fire. The couple next door who usually try to regularly check on her were out of town that week. They're pretty cut up about not being around."

"Investigation of the warehouse fire scene is ongoing," Greyson said, then passed it over to Captain Tennet.

Tennet peered at the papers in front of him. "We have gone through about fifty percent of the structure so far. The team is at work on it now, contractors who understand evidence cleanup procedures. But early yesterday morning when we first walked the scene—"

"You secured it?" Julio asked.

Tennet nodded. "It's safe."

Julio nodded. That was good. He wanted to walk through the scene where he'd almost lost his life. It was something he'd been taught to do as a rookie. Memories lived in your head, and in a tense situation that turned to a nightmare quickly, they could build and build in the mind of a firefighter. Until the memory of an incident became more powerful than what had actually happened.

If he walked through the debris in the light of day, his fear would diminish.

Julio said, "Thanks."

Tennet knew why. They came from the same training school, similar eras of firefighting. Even if they'd gone two different directions as captains in the Benson Fire Department. "Yesterday, we found a deceased person in a back room at the warehouse."

Julio frowned. "I thought we got everyone out?"

"We did as well," Greyson said. The chief would take responsibility, but only because Julio had broken protocol and gone inside, forcing him to take command of the scene.

"The deceased was discovered in a back room," the captain continued. "Apparently, the staff were present for a meeting, and this guy is the lawyer. They actually said they weren't aware he'd arrived yet."

Someone only just got there when the fire started. Didn't that mean there would have been indications of smoke, or heat. They'd have had time to get out, surely?

"Accelerant?" Julio asked.

"We're running tests. I'll pass on the results."

That was new. Arson didn't usually invite outside help in their cases. In fact, they played things extremely close to the vest. What were Samantha and her partner doing here? He wanted to lift his hands, sign to her and ask, but he was already looking at possible suspension.

Samantha said, "Did any of the employees indicate why they were meeting after hours?"

Tennet shook his head. "We couldn't get them to say, but we're still working through initial interviews. The parent company had no idea why they were meeting."

Samantha picked up her pen and made a note on the pad in front of her. "I'll add that to my list to find out, after we connect the dots on the lawyer."

"Could be something fishy," Romeo said. "The arsonist knew what the meeting was going to be about, set everything up, and timed it so they'd be there."

Julio figured it was a decent theory. "Are you taking the case?"

Greyson cleared his throat. "Actually, you all are."

A taskforce. Seriously? But the chance to work with

Samantha... Even if Romeo was there, it was more contact than he'd had with her in months. Years, even. Would it change anything for them to be colleagues for a while?

"As of now, the people in this room comprise our newest interagency taskforce." Greyson glanced at Samantha and Romeo. "We know you have other cases. Most of the personnel in here will be doing double duty..."

Samantha picked it up. "But with two deaths now, and lives at risk, it needs to be priority." She paused. "Maybe someone in the fire department brass can speak with the police commissioner. Get at least myself reassigned for the duration. Detective Alvarez can float back and forth as needed."

Greyson nodded. "I like that idea." He looked at Julio, a question on his face.

Julio didn't have a problem with it, so he said nothing. Working with Samantha on a case? He wanted the people in this city to feel safe, but he also wanted to see her more. Hang out. Spend time together. All those expressions that basically meant the same thing.

The chance at giving it another shot.

Or, at least being able to talk about the idea.

He tried to gauge if she agreed but couldn't tell. She'd always been able to keep her emotions below the surface, until she started to sign and her face lit up with expression.

"I'll go speak with my sergeant." She gathered her things and stood.

The meeting was breaking up, so Julio timed it so he went to the door at the same time she did. Her partner right behind her.

"You look a lot better than the last time we saw you," Romeo said.

Julio held his hand out, and Romeo shook it. "Thanks. I feel a whole lot better."

"You really think there's an arsonist out there?"

"Guess it's our job to find out. Shut him down."

Samantha turned, in the hall now. "Like that guy... what was it, twenty years ago? I remember watching a TV special on it."

He knew exactly what she was talking about. "Wanna meet up later. Compare notes?"

Samantha lifted her chin, just a fraction, but he knew what it meant before she said, "I'm not sure there's anything to say."

Romeo wandered off down the hall. Probably sensing the tension in the air and wanting nothing to do with something that had already turned personal.

"Sam—"

She shook her head. "I believe you already made your point loud and clear."

Then she walked away.

EIGHT

Samantha kept her focus on her computer monitor, even though out the corner of her eye she saw Romeo glance over every now and again. Like he wanted to say something.

But what was there to say?

Julio...

She couldn't even get into that kiss. What was the point? It wasn't like anything had changed. Not then, and not now. She wanted to ask him what he was playing at, but this wasn't about games and he'd never been like that anyway.

Her phone buzzed with another text from her sister, but she ignored it. Kept working.

A cup of coffee was set down in front of her.

She tipped her head to the side and eyed Romeo. "Thanks?"

"Fine. It's not a peace offering. I want to know." He circled the end of their desks and sat back down at his, opposite her.

They weren't the only ones in the office right now. An

older detective sat at his desk, headphones on. Probably making notes from a recorded interview. The sergeant was in her office with the door closed.

Even if no one was around to hear, she still didn't exactly want to talk about it. Far easier to pretend the past hadn't happened. Social media said to live in the now, sucked into scrolling through other people's content. Not living her own life in the real world. She liked to disassociate as much as the next person. Sometimes with this job, it was entirely necessary to disappear into funny cat videos and snippets from comedians.

It could save a person's sanity, in fact.

Pretty much anything was better than getting dragged back into the past, even just in her mind.

"Tell me what happened between you and Julio."

Samantha held on to her mug, trying to warm her hands. Elbows tight to her sides. She probably looked like a victim, being interviewed after major trauma. "We were together."

Romeo studied her. "For how long?" he finally asked.

"Years. A lot of years. We met in middle school. We stuck together, because both of us didn't quite fit in the hearing world and we didn't really fit in deaf culture either. So we carved out our own subset of each, and we lived there together all through school. I went to college, and he fought wildfires in Alaska for a while. We drifted in different directions and saw other people. I did, anyway. I never asked if he saw someone else. After I'd been a cop for a few months, we bumped into each other on a callout. He was back here, with the fire department in Benson."

Their relationship had been like a dormant fire that came to life again in a flash.

Ignition.

"It was hot and heavy, and we were at least talking about getting married." She winced. Probably too much information, but he had to know where her morals began and ended, or they'd never fully trust each other as partners.

"Until what?"

"The day we got blown up, actually." Samantha stared at the coffee. "I took a pregnancy test that morning. I went by the station because he was at work and told him in person. But we didn't get to make any plans. I was due in for my shift, and he had a callout."

"And that was the day you were thrown out of the house. You got a concussion, didn't you?"

She nodded.

"And you..."

"Lost the baby." She drew in a shuddering breath.

"I'm sorry for your loss. That must've been..." Romeo winced. "I can't even imagine."

"Neither of us took it well, but I could only manage myself. I didn't want to talk to anyone, so I had my sister tell him to leave. He came back a couple of times, then came over to the house later. And days after that. Whenever he could." She sniffed and cleared her throat.

The tears had been spent two years ago, but still every time she remembered it they gathered fresh in her eyes. Burning with the pain of the past. The way a fire scorched skin when you least expected it. Like when she reached for a pan she forgot was hot from the oven.

It had taken time, but she'd worked her way through it. Julio must have as well in the ensuing two years. But despite the grief that had torn them apart, it seemed clear he might still feel the same way.

Still, her mind insisted she remember that day. Tears streaming down both their faces, they'd screamed at each other in her living room. Pleaded. Yelled—until her sister came in and flipped the lights on and off to get them to stop. "He wanted to be there for me, but I told him to never come back. It was pretty ugly."

"You were in pain." Romeo paused. "He knew that, right?"

She shut her eyes and nodded. "He knew. But I told him not to come back, so he didn't." And she'd regretted it ever since.

"He obviously cares about you still. That says something, after all this time."

But that didn't mean there was anything she could do about it. Far better to just let things lie and move on. She could handle herself. She liked her job, and her apartment with her sister was nice. She was saving for a house, and she'd have the downpayment soon—give or take when the market felt like going down again.

Romeo pressed his lips together.

He had an opinion, but wasn't sure she wanted to hear it? She knew the guy decently. Not well enough to be totally sure on reading him. The only person she'd ever been able to fully read was Julio. Even her boyfriend in senior year of college had been a mystery to her. She'd never kept it a secret that she wanted to be a cop. Then he went and acted all surprised. As if her choice said something about him and he wasn't interested in how it made him look with a cop as a girlfriend.

"My sister would say God is doing something," Romeo continued. "If things seem like they're changing, then maybe it's because He's at work."

"Is He?" She'd never experienced anything like that

before. Seemed more like she lived her life, and God was just God. He was the Creator in the sky, a Father she had rarely felt a need to connect with. "How am I supposed to know what He's doing, or what He wants?"

"Read the Bible. Go to church?" He shrugged. "I'm not the best at this, so I don't know. Can it be simple? Sometimes I think we overcomplicate things because we need it to be difficult rather than just letting go."

Samantha drank some more of her coffee. "I should get back to this research." She wanted to find out as much as she could about the elderly woman who'd been the first victim. Do her job. Focus on what she could control, rather than what felt like it was trying to spin her into the earth's orbit. Talk about being off her axis. She was going to work the case, because if there was an arsonist out there...

Safe to say the idea scared her enough she wanted to focus hard and figure this out before things got any worse. Before someone else got hurt or killed. The way Julio could've been the other night.

"Before you disappear into the job again..."

She looked at Romeo, one brow raised. Her heart squeezing hard in her chest.

"...when did you learn sign language?"

"I learned it when the rest of my family did." She forced her face to remain impassive. "My sister is deaf."

"Your sister." He stared at her, a questioning look on his face.

Was he putting the pieces together? He wouldn't be much of a detective if it didn't even cross his mind that was who she'd been with at the diner. Samantha studied his expression, but he turned to his computer and grabbed the mouse.

"Huh," was all he said. Then, "That's cool."

He might be acting all smooth about it, like it was no big deal. But she figured the first chance he got, Romeo would be looking up her next of kin trying to get her sister's name. After that, he'd do a search on social media and promptly discover her sister ran a local group that connected members of the deaf community with services and events that were geared toward them.

She figured by Friday he'd have found her sister's number without her giving it to him.

But he would still want to know if Bristol had asked about him.

Never in a million years would Samantha tell him that her sister had been asking about him daily since the diner. Questioning her about her new partner, and what he was like. If he was single.

"Jesse!"

Samantha glanced over at the open doorway.

Sergeant Megan Deerdan had one hand on the frame, only her head and the shoulders of her blouse out the door. "I'm losing you to Arson at the fire department?"

"I guess so, Sergeant."

Deerdan nodded. "Good idea."

Okay, then.

The sergeant started to go back in her office, but jerked her head back out. "Oh, and I got an email from the chief. You're up for a commendation for your actions in the diner the other day. So good job."

"Thanks."

Deerdan disappeared back in her office.

"A commendation. That's great."

Samantha wasn't sure she agreed with Romeo's assessment.

"It's...not great?"

She shrugged. "Can't stop it. Can't turn it down. Why worry about what will happen whether you like it or not?"

"It's a good thing. You might get a medal."

"I'd rather close this case."

"So you're the ultimate. A cop's cop. Only in it for the satisfaction of justice. No glory, no recognition."

Samantha pressed her lips together. "If you think about whether you might get a commendation or if you'll end up in handcuffs, it affects your judgment. In the heat of the moment, you hesitate or choose differently than what training or instinct tell you to."

"Okay, I get that." He lifted his coffee mug, looking disappointed, then took a sip and set it down. "But don't you want someone to tell you that you did a good job at least?"

"I'm the one that knows if I did a good job, or not." Because she knew her own intentions. She needed to look in the mirror and see a person with integrity, someone she could respect.

"So you just work?"

"What else is there to do?"

"We need to go shoot some pool later," Romeo suggested. "*Something*. Better yet, I'll ask Julio to come. And you ask your sister. We'll all go hang out."

She focused on her computer monitor. "I'm busy."

Romeo chuckled.

She smiled but didn't look at him. So he'd figured it out. She wasn't about to hang out with Julio just so Romeo could get to know her sister. If he wanted to do that, he'd have to learn sign language. She wasn't going to interpret for him.

If a man wanted to pursue a woman, he had to do the work.

The way Julio had relentlessly shown up every day to walk her to the school bus. He'd pretty much claimed her and never let go. Until she forced his hand.

If Romeo wanted to convince Bristol he was interested enough to be serious, it was up to him to do it. He didn't have to prove he was worthy of her. More like that he considered her worth the effort it would take to win her over.

As for her and Julio...

Different thing entirely.

Life always seemed to tear them apart. But when they came back together, they were all-in. Julio might have intentionally staked his claim at that fire scene, whether he'd been fully in control of himself or not. He'd made the first move.

If anything was going to happen, it was up to her to take the next step.

Or walk away for good.

NINE

Richard pushed a shopping cart down the aisle in the big box hardware store, more proof that multinational corporations took all the heart out of retail. This stuff was generic and poorly made, as though all this company cared about was making as much off the consumer as possible.

Gone were the days of quality workmanship, integrity in business, or caring about the customer.

Things just weren't the same anymore. Not like they used to be.

He added a couple of tubes of caulk to his cart, beside the insulation and duct tape. A couple of PVC pipes, and he should be done.

Richard found those easily enough. The employee with the vest who was on his phone didn't even offer to help him find what he was looking for.

When he rolled up to the checkout, the attendant made eye contact. "How's it going?"

Richard had to be perfectly unremarkable. Thanks to genetics, he figured it worked. The man he looked like right now was a nobody in a line of nobodies that came through here. Even if the police talked to the cashier, he probably wouldn't be able to remember much about Richard.

"Fine, thanks." He nodded, then turned away to shift items in his cart so the guy could scan each one. "How's it going with you?"

Beep. "Can't complain." *Beep.* "Friday, so not as bad as it could be."

"Exactly."

"Got any plans for the weekend?" The cashier looked around his cart. "Looks like an interesting job."

"Couple of different ones, actually."

The guy nodded. "Makes sense."

"Just some odd jobs around town."

"Handyman. Nice." The guy rang him up.

Richard paid with cash so it left no record. The police wouldn't bother running fingerprint tests. Too much work on the off chance they'd be able to find his print on a bill—which they wouldn't. The results would just net them a bunch of partials, and random matches that made no sense and would take days or weeks to sort through.

"Here you go."

He accepted the change and the receipt. "Thanks."

With any luck, this man would barely remember him. Any security footage would show a guy at least fifty pounds heavier than him, with completely different hair. No shot of his earlobes, so they wouldn't be able to ID him that way.

He knew what the police and the feds could do. And though he'd drawn the line at prosthetics, it didn't matter. They had no way to find him. No trace. No leads. No hope of stopping him.

Everything had been designed to outsmart them, and he would succeed.

Richard pushed the cart out, through the sliding doors. The line for the food truck outside stretched nearly in front of the doors. He shoved around a couple of guys who looked like landscapers and headed for his car.

The bland gold-colored car would need to be changed out for a new shade within a few days. It had served its purpose, but keeping it much longer was too risky.

He turned the engine on, flipping the air-conditioning to full blast so it could cool the car while he loaded the stuff in the back. When he was done, he sat in the driver's seat and eased the little notebook out of his pocket. He crossed off everything he'd bought and wrote down the final totals.

He'd underestimated the cost. He was going to run out of the old lady's funds if he wasn't careful with how much he drove.

Gas prices these days. It's enough to make a guy crazy.

Richard's own amusement reached his ears when he hadn't even realized he'd been laughing.

No more trips to look at the wreckage he'd caused, the burned-out buildings that were now symbols of what he could achieve.

Okay, maybe one quick look at the last one.

He'd figure out how to get some cash together another way. The old lady had been useful, but she'd served her purpose and that was done. He wondered if any of the others would turn out to be hiding money under their mattresses.

He could hope.

Right now, Richard wanted to see what he had achieved. His hands shook as he drove there, the curly strands of the wig flicked against his face as the air-conditioning vent moved the air around. A couple of blocks away from the hardware store, he'd tugged off the hair and scrubbed a hand over his scalp. His rough hand scratched across the skin on top of his head, and the strands around the sides that remained.

The spot where he'd had skin cancer a few years ago. The counselor he'd seen at the time told him to find his passion, to try to dedicate the rest of his life to meaningful work that fulfilled him.

And here we are.

He pulled over to the curb, close enough he could see the warehouse from this spot. Police tape blocked off the whole area, and technicians were still going through every inch of it. As if they would figure out his true motive. They could search and search, and still they wouldn't find him in the center of anything. He was a ghost, a remnant of the past. And he would be up until it all came together, and he completed the task.

He felt his lips curl up, just thinking about the master plan he had in the works. How the police and that new arson investigation team they'd put together would be spinning their wheels trying to figure out who he was.

By the time they did, it would be far too late. He would have what he wanted.

Ascension.

He would become the best version of himself. The ultimate.

The truth.

TEN

"Go ahead and catch us up to speed, Detective Jesse." Across the other side of the conference room table, Captain Tennet picked up his pen.

Julio glanced at the clock, which indicated it wasn't quite seven in the morning. Still, Samantha didn't look nearly as tired as he felt. Maybe she just slept better than he had last night. All that tossing and turning trying to figure out what to say to her next. He should have been working on this case, but instead, being in proximity with her just brought back to reality the strength of their connection. How thoroughly connected to her he was. How much she'd always been under his skin.

Across the table, she tapped the screen of a tablet. "Thank you, Captain. The elderly woman who died in the second fire you already know was Eva Bronswich, eighty-four years old and a lifelong resident of Benson. What you might not know was that she changed her name years ago, legally going back to her maiden name. As a married woman, she was Eva Sylvana."

Julio frowned. He glanced around at the others, seeing similar looks on several faces.

He knew that name.

"If you recognize the surname, that's because it belongs to Richard Sylvana. Convicted of several counts of arson and murder nearly twenty years ago now, the sentence for which he is currently serving. And where he will remain for probably the rest of his life."

Captain Tennet shook his head. "The first victim of our arsonist was that arsonist's mother?"

Julio knew the look on Samantha's face. She had more.

"Now we get to the lawyer from the warehouse fire. The deceased didn't always work in corporate law. At one point he was a criminal attorney, namely the lawyer who represented one Richard Sylvana."

Tennet muttered something under his breath.

Julio might agree, but he wasn't about to express it like that. Besides, he was far more interested in that look on Samantha's face. The way her eyes lit up as she ran down the details of the case. She had always loved what she did. No matter what it was, she only did things she believed in. That meant when she was busy working, she put her whole heart and soul into what she was doing.

And the satisfaction she got out of it was plain on her face.

Once upon a time, he had put that look on her face as well, the one that made her seem so much brighter. The passing of the baby they had created together had stolen that light from her, but she seemed to have figured out how to get at least some of it back.

He wanted to figure out how to see the expression of pure joy on her face again—because of him. Not just for the sake of bringing the past back to life, but because she deserved to have that much happiness. Maybe she didn't want it with him now. He might have to accept that it was too late. But the truth was, he'd never been able to let go of her.

He knew she had lost a partner in the last year. Did she want some of that joy again?

"Captain Espinoza-Vasquez?"

He blinked and realized Tennet was talking to him. "Sorry, what was that?"

Across the table, Romeo Alvarez smirked—though it did seem good-natured. Julio wanted to ball up the paper in front of him and toss it at the guy's head. Samantha didn't make eye contact with him. Though he could see a red blush to her cheeks.

Maybe he was making more progress than he thought.

Kissing her off the bat, just to make a point? That might have backfired. But no one could deny it was a simple way for everyone to know where he was at.

Tennet said, "You've made amazing progress, detectives. Please continue. We can come back to what Captain Espinoza-Vasquez has afterward."

Romeo said, "When I spoke with the company, they reluctantly explained they are getting ready for a fight with a group of disgruntled customers who believed they received faulty equipment. The company supplies machinery to dry cleaners. We are going to work with the court case angle and try to see if the fire might have been started by any of the plaintiffs."

Beside him, Samantha said, "The fire was set to destroy the building and their people. If one of the plaintiffs is the suspect, then all they achieve is potentially destroying evidence. The company files on their insurance for the building and gets paid. It might mean that the lawsuit goes nowhere, wrecking the case. Possibly on top of that, the company ends up ahead thanks to the insurance payout."

"So you don't think it was one of the plaintiffs?" Julio asked.

She shook her head. "It's a longshot, but we have to rule out what isn't as much as trying to ascertain what *was*."

Julio could understand that. "One of the plaintiffs in the case would have no reason to commit the other crimes, right? There would be no reason for them to set the other fires and kill the mother of an arsonist from years ago."

"No reason that we know of," she said. "The connection is too abstract, which means it's likely a case of figuring out which it is."

Tennet nodded. "So what's next, Captain?"

"Testing from all the scenes is ongoing," Julio said. "But I went out to the warehouse yesterday and managed to confirm the ventilation system was blocked. Someone purposely prevented airflow to maximize the smoke buildup inside the building."

"Sabotage by the arsonists, or poor maintenance in the warehouse?" Romeo asked.

"That's what I need to find out next. Probably by talking to the same people you're talking to." Though, he'd rather go with Samantha to speak to people than go with her partner. No offense to Romeo Alvarez, but his partner was much better looking.

Samantha said, "Romeo has interviews set up with the plaintiffs. I'm going to the jail to talk to Richard Sylvana."

Julio sat up straighter in his seat. "I'll go with you."

He started to pack away his things, along with everyone else. No way was he going to pass up this opportunity to spend several hours in a row with Samantha. Most of it in a car where she couldn't run away from whatever questions he had.

But that wasn't the tactic he needed to take.

Could he breach the anger he'd felt toward God for so long, enough to figure out how to ask for wisdom with Samantha? Sure, he'd gone to church over the years when he could. He always told people he was a believer, and on the surface he probably seemed like a guy who did the right thing and didn't swear all the time like a lot of the firefighters did.

Underneath the surface, his faith had been hollow for a long time.

In order to get Samantha back in his life, hopefully this time for good, he might just have to do the work to make his belief genuine. Rely on God. Though, even that was a gamble when he took into account God's will. Maybe the Lord had been working years ago when they broke up, and they weren't supposed to be together.

Maybe he was supposed to have moved on.

But instead, he'd held on to his feelings for her, almost as though he'd moved on from God.

Julio winced.

Samantha said, "Everything okay?"

"Sure." The most benign, nothing word in the world. But it served his purpose, walking alongside her to where he'd parked his truck.

"I know you just assumed that you'd be the one driving, but I appreciate the ride. That way I don't leave Romeo without a car."

He stopped by the passenger side and opened the door for her. "You're welcome."

She shook her head, actually smiling.

When he got in on the other side, he decided that rather than keep the banter going he would let her have the security of just talking about work. "So tell me what you know about this arsonist guy. We were pretty young when it all went down. But I remember it being in the news and on the newspapers we used that summer when we went camping without telling our parents."

She chuckled. "It was freezing, and the tent had a hole in it. I do remember you used the newspaper to light a fire."

"What else was I going to do? Your teeth were chattering." He'd had a good time, but the moment they were back from the park the next morning both of their parents had been at her house. The two of them had been in serious trouble for only telling Samantha's sister where they were going. "How is Bristol these days?"

"Oh, she's fine."

Julio glanced over. "What does that mean?"

He realized that instead of talking about work they had slipped into something personal—their shared history. Because God had led their conversation this way? Julio was willing to concede being in control of everything. Especially if God gave him the desires of his heart.

He just wasn't convinced his motives were pure enough God would honor that.

Samantha sighed. "I'm just balancing everything. Trying not to let work and my personal life overlap."

And here he was, determined to convince her to give him another shot. "Is it so bad if there's a little crossover?"

"I like my life segmented. I prefer it when everything

stays in its lane, and I can manage, rather than it all being messy and complicated."

Okay, so that was progress at least. "Complicated doesn't always mean bad, and neither does messy. Sometimes things are chaotic in a good way."

"And sometimes we just need to focus on thing in front of us—a case involving an arsonist who has committed more than one murder." She kept her focus on the road in front of them, the way he probably should be doing.

"And when the case is done?"

She didn't answer his question, and Julio wasn't going to push her to do so. She flipped through the dials on his radio and found a soft rock station she put on low while he drove them to the jail.

He left the volume where it was but said, "I still need an answer to my original question."

She stiffened.

"What do you know about this arsonist guy?" It wasn't like he'd ever interviewed a suspect before, and he certainly hadn't visited anyone in jail. The last time he'd been out here it was because half the building had exploded in another bomb attack.

Another suspect at another time. The same person who had been responsible for her partner's death in the drive-by shooting that took out more than a few cops after a fake funeral.

He'd been called in because he headed up the bomb squad in Benson. Not that they were official, or anything.

"Oh," she said. "Right, Richard Sylvana. He's in his sixties now. He had skin cancer a few years ago, but received treatment for it in prison and is in remission now."

"Is he likely to answer any of our questions?" Julio paused. "Do people in prison do that? Or do they get shanked or whatever for talking to the cops?"

She chuckled lightly. "It's up to him if he talks to us. We can't compel him to answer any questions. This is just a friendly chat."

"I'm not feeling very friendly toward a guy who murdered people and set fires."

"We need him to be friendly. We're going to be professional."

"Right." Julio figured he could do that.

At least for a while.

After that, the case would be closed, and all bets would be off. If Samantha thought before that she understood his point loud and clear, she would definitely not mistake his intentions then.

He wanted her back in his life.

ELEVEN

Samantha knew exactly what Julio was doing. There was never anything about him that she wasn't aware of, simply because they had known each other for so long. Sure, it might have been a while since they hung out with any regularity, but Julio was the epitome of all those metaphors about oak trees that withstood the test of time.

She'd clung to him for so long that once she became untethered, she'd been forced to find a new anchor.

Her job.

Now it seemed as though he wanted to participate in that with her. And the moment the case was done, she knew he would be full throttle about getting back together with her.

She walked down the hallway of the prison, following one of the uniformed officers. Julio behind her. Samantha didn't dare glance back. If she did, she would only be reminded of exactly how enticing he had always been to her.

The man was the definition of tall, dark, and handsome.

Or, as Bristol put it, *fiiiiine*. That long drawn-out sign she had made up, mixing the sign for Julio's name with that word. Giving him a designation that was all his own.

Pure Julio.

He was the reason her sister had a complex about romance, waiting for the day she would be swept off her feet. But not by Romeo Alvarez. At least as far as Samantha could make sure that never happened.

Samantha had given up romantic dreams a long time ago.

They were hardly necessary when her job brought her up against the worst of the worst in Benson, crimes that most people wouldn't even be able to handle knowing about. And small dingy interview rooms in jails. Currently occupied by a single table, two chairs, and an older man chained to the floor wearing an orange jumpsuit.

The officer said, "I'll stay out here."

"Thanks." She eased into the room with Julio behind her, wearing his firefighter uniform of thick blue cargoes and a light-blue polo shirt, his radio across from one shoulder to his hip. The bars of his captain rank on his shoulders. Meanwhile, she had on her every day nothing special uniform of suit pants and a blouse.

Her badge on her belt.

Her gun safely locked away with the officer on the front desk, along with her electronics.

She tugged out the chair and sat, while Julio folded his arms and leaned against the wall. "I'm Detective Jesse. This is Captain Espinoza-Vasquez from the fire department."

How would Richard Sylvana react to hearing about a spate of fires recently, deaths and mayhem committed by one person?

Maybe she needed to gently break the news of his mother's passing. Or his lawyer.

"I don't care about fires anymore," he muttered. His saggy cheeks shifted when he spoke, his jowls hanging down on the sides of his face. "I've been receiving treatment, and now I'm cured of my obsession with heat and flames." His flat eyes didn't betray anything other than truth in the words he spoke.

"Your mother's name is Eva, is that correct?"

He flinched, and a little of the façade cracked.

"I'm sorry to have to tell you, but she passed away recently."

"She was old. We all go some point."

Julio said, "Most of us aren't the victims of a fire that's the result of arson."

She studied Richard's response to that, watching for indications he might know something. When she couldn't discern anything specific, she said, "I also have to tell you, unfortunately, that the lawyer who represented you in your trial all those years ago was also the victim of a different fire. But also arson. We believe the two are connected."

Richard looked at Julio, then back at her. "Insulation in the ducting where it shouldn't be? HVAC blockages so that the smoke has nowhere to go?"

"How about weakened structures to aid in the collapse of the building?" Julio said.

"And victims carefully chosen," Samantha added. "Though, this last one had potentially collateral damage.

Unless the arsonist intended to kill everyone in that meeting."

Richard sat back in his chair. "How should I know? I've been in here for twenty years."

"Don't worry. We'll see who has been visiting you." She watched his eyes flare, and decided they also needed to check into mail he had received or sent. Everything was opened and checked. Every letter and package the inmate received went through close scrutiny.

If there was something to find, she was going to find it.

"Whoever he is," Julio said, "he's using your tactics. The tricks of your trade that you honed over all those years. Wouldn't you want to know who it is that's trying to steal your thunder?"

Richard shrugged one shoulder. "What's to steal? I have nothing, and like I said, I don't care about fire anymore."

Samantha decided to try a different angle. One that wasn't exactly on the table, but she could work out the details later if necessary.

"This guy knows everything about you," she told him. "Which means you know exactly what kind of person he is. You could have valuable intel that will help us catch him before he kills someone else."

Assuming Richard even cared enough to want to do the right thing.

But she had more leverage than just counting on his goodwill.

"If you provide us with information that leads to his capture, I can speak with the district attorney and find out what kind of concessions you might be able to receive. Rewards for good behavior. Maybe even a reduced sentence so you can see the light of day before you're past being able to enjoy it."

She was aware Julio had shifted. No surprise he didn't like what she was saying, but he also didn't object to it here. He had always trusted her ability to do her job, and she was counting on that trust right now.

This was a negotiation. As much as cops didn't want to make it so, often interviews were nothing but a battle of wills on who could outsmart the other. She had always liked the thrill of figuring out how to persuade a suspect to talk to her.

Becoming a detective might have been at least in part about not being a beat cop anymore. But also, changing the direction of her career trajectory had been more about working cases than responding to calls. Getting her out of walking the beat where she had no idea what she would be responding to on any given day. Like entering a house and seconds later a bomb going off.

Now that she did the job, she knew she had the skills to do it well. She might even go so far as to say that being a detective was what she had been born to do.

Too bad being a cop had cost her everything else that was good in her life.

"And when anyone in here finds out I'm cooperating with the police?" He huffed out a laugh. "What do I care what happens on the outside? The only thing I've got left is me." He thumped a hand on his chest. "And I'm not getting killed for trying to skate out of my sentence."

Some cops, at this juncture, might start to threaten to take away what concessions he had already worked in for himself. The freedoms he had in this place. They might convince him they had the power to throw him in solitary for weeks at a time.

As far as Samantha was concerned, no one deserved inhumane treatment. Not even criminals.

"Then answer me one question before I go."

Richard waited.

"First, your mother dies. Then your lawyer. So who's next?" She paused. "If it was you, who would be next on the list?"

He studied her, probably thinking through his answer. Although if she had to guess she would say he already knew exactly who would be next.

The judge?

The arson investigator who had testified against him years ago, or one of the original investigating detectives, maybe?

Could be this current arsonist was planning on picking off every single member of the jury that had convicted Richard Sylvana twenty years ago.

Richard leaned slightly forward, a predatory smile on his face. "Have fun figuring it out." He sat back in the chair and chuckled to himself.

"Come on." Julio tapped her on the side of her arm. "Let's go."

Samantha stared down Richard for a few more seconds, then pushed the chair back and stood. He didn't need to believe that Julio was in charge. That lowered her in his eyes, diminishing his perception of her authority.

Julio didn't know that. Or didn't consider it to be that big of a deal considering this guy would never be able to even touch her. However, in order for her to get her work done, somebody like Richard had to believe she had all the authority in the room.

"One more thing." She turned back, leaning one fist on the table. "You have a son, don't you?"

She saw the tiny flinch in his eyes.

"I'll tell him you said hi."

She turned and walked to the door, following Julio out into the hall. As soon as the door clicked shut, he said, "What was that about his son?"

"I needed a way to put him off balance, since he felt as if he ended with the upper hand. Now, next time I come in, he won't be so sure of himself."

Before Julio could say anything else, the warden approached them. His dress shoes clicked on the tile floor. Julio shook his hand, then said, "This is Detective Jesse. Samantha, this is Warden Bernstein."

"Nice to meet you." She shook his hand as well. "I'd like to talk about who visited Richard Sylvana over the years and if he has received or sent any mail."

Warden Bernstein nodded. "I have an administrative assistant compiling all of that for you now. He's only had a couple of visitors over the years. His mother, once or twice. A couple of reporters looking for a story, and a psychologist from the local university doing a research paper."

"What about any letters or packages?" Samantha asked.

"We have documentation of everything that was sent and received. But it's his incoming mail you're going to want to take a look at."

Julio said, "You have it?"

Warden Bernstein nodded. "While you had him in the interview room, we went through his cell and retrieved everything."

Samantha wasn't sure that was entirely above board. If Richard got himself a lawyer, he could probably argue an illegal search and seizure. Didn't cell searches have to be pre-announced? She should find out. But if it saved lives? Warden Bernstein would have to be prepared to answer for his actions.

Bernstein led them to an open plan office with several desks. On top of one was a stack of letters. "They appear to be fan mail. For the most part they are one offs, random letters from people reaching out to Richard."

"And the rest?" Samantha was all too aware of Julio standing beside her.

This had to be a test. If Romeo was right that God was doing something in her life, then the only possible thing she could think was that He was determined to test her resolve. To make sure she was really living the way she believed she should.

The warden lifted a letter and handed it to her.

"I'll need to secure all these in evidence bags." But she looked at it without touching the paper, seeing hand-written words on the page.

I have not yet shown you who I am. But one day you will see me. For I will become as you are, and then so much more.

Reborn in the flames.

The arsonist had reached out to Richard, his idol. Now he was killing people connected to Sylvana's case. Those who had failed him, perhaps?

Julio said, "We need to find this guy before he kills someone else."

He was right. At least about this.

They would see what else he was right about. Things she didn't have the bandwidth to worry about when an arsonist was out there, looking for someone else to kill.

Time was running out.

TWELVE

Julio had been in the Benson Police Department before, but never in the office of the Intelligence division. It probably wouldn't be a surprise to anyone that he much preferred the homey feel of the firehouse. After all, as firefighters he and his colleagues spent so much time in their station that they had to make it feel like a home away from home. Bunk rooms, common room, and a full kitchen.

Then again, cops didn't come to work and spend hours asleep until it was time to go out and respond to a call. The nature of their jobs was different, but in the end they both served the community. Meeting people on the worst day of their life and extending a hand to help them.

He carried the stack of water bottles in his hands from the break room Samantha had pointed out back to their "bullpen," as she'd called it. No bigger than the kitchen and living area at the firehouse, they had packed eight desks in here, most of them back-to-back. File cabinets lining the walls. A huge cork board on wheels.

He was pretty sure that those pictures up there weren't meant for him to see.

A fact he was certain of when he stepped back into the room and saw Romeo turning the board around to face the wall. The top edge obscured the bottom of the TV screen hung at the top of the wall. Playing one of those 24/7 news stations, but this one currently had a local feed being broadcast.

Julio stacked the waters on the table where Samantha had her laptop open and sat in front of it speaking with a blonde on the screen. FBI special agent Addie Franklin, the niece of the police commissioner, was at home. Or so he figured, since she had blurred out her background.

"This is going to be a rough one, I can tell you that much," Addie said.

"I appreciate you taking a look at the letters. There isn't anyone else in Benson who is trained in behavioral analysis the way you are." Samantha took one of the waters and shot him a grateful smile.

Julio was too antsy to sit after all the driving they'd done to the jail and back, so he wandered to the windows and looked out through the vertical blinds.

The afternoon sun bounced off the glass windows of the building across the street, creating a glare that made him wince. Below them, traffic streamed in both directions. He didn't come downtown to headquarters that much. He had once entertained the thought of living in a high-rise and biking to work. Now, he knew that would never fit him.

Did Samantha even know where he lived?

Maybe showing her would be a point on his scorecard.

Through the laptop speakers, Addie said, "I will need

to keep studying them to get a truly full picture of the type of guy this is. And I may send one of my agents to you if you need a hand. Don't hesitate to ask."

Did that mean she thought this was serious?

"So you think this guy will turn even deadlier than he already is?" Samantha asked.

Julio smiled at the window.

"What you have is some serious pathology," Addie replied. "There are religious undertones to these letters. Which indicates he likely is someone who had a conservative upbringing."

Julio made a sound low in his throat.

Addie continued, "But then he's also delusional and dangerous. It's almost as if he sees himself as connected to Richard. Maybe bonded in some way? And then in some of these, it almost seems like he thinks he *is* him."

Julio turned from the window. Samantha looked at him, and he signed, *What does that mean?*

To Addie she said, "Any idea what that means?" The corners of her lips curled up slightly.

Romeo wandered back over from tidying, all so Julio didn't see anything sensitive connected to an Intelligence Division or Major Crimes case.

"Give me some more time with this," Addie said. "Let me unpack it a little, and I'll get back to you first thing tomorrow." In the background of the connection, a baby started to cry. "Good timing."

"Thank you, Special Agent Franklin."

"No problem, Detective." They ended the video call, and Samantha closed her laptop. She let out a breath, smoothing back her hair and tucking it behind her ears. She'd left it down, but he knew she liked to put in a ponytail when it started to irritate her. She had a hair tie on one wrist. Probably for later, just in case.

Romeo pulled out a chair and sat across from her. He glanced at Julio while he did the same. "Let me guess, you have a thing about 'conservative' upbringings?"

Right. He'd made that noise in his throat. "I just don't like people who give other people a bad name. The last thing the world needs is criminals who are crazy religious when faith is supposed to make you a better person. It's not supposed to justify your psychosis."

"Hmm." Romeo reached for a bottled water. "You might have a point."

Julio said, "Seems to me like it doesn't depend on the values themselves. It depends on the nature of the person instilling it in you. A narcissist and a nun might believe the same things, but they will teach the lesson in two very different ways."

Samantha studied him. "It's not the sword. It's the one who wields it."

Romeo said, "What was it like having two deaf parents? If it's okay for me to ask."

Julio nodded. "From my earliest memories, I can recall having to interpret the world for them. Relaying communication back and forth between them and the hearing world. Like a bridge between the two."

"Might not be too different from a child of immigrants brought up in a different country than the culture their parents belong to."

"I think it's probably similar. Especially if their native language is different and they aren't able to learn the language of the culture they live in." At least a hearing person could make the attempt to assimilate and learn a new language. But if they didn't, it might have no bearing on how they felt about the place where they lived.

"That's a lot to put on a kid." Romeo looked at him with a little bit of something like respect.

Julio shrugged. His upbringing had never given him a high opinion of himself. He just had an inbuilt need to slow down and make sure everyone around him understood what was being said. "It was all I knew. And you don't resent things until you understand what isn't right about a situation. Or what you don't have, but maybe should."

He had let go of it—if he'd ever had any frustration in the first place.

He looked at Samantha. "I've had to learn how to let go of a lot of things. Life has taught me what's worth holding on to and what wasn't."

Samantha cleared her throat. "How are your parents?"

"Really good," he said. "The community where they live in Florida is great for them."

Romeo snorted. "Shame about the hurricanes and the alligators."

Julio smiled.

Romeo's attention caught on something behind Julio's back, and he pushed his chair back and stood. So fast that the chair toppled over behind him. The look on his face...

Samantha said under her breath, "Oh, no."

Julio twisted around in the seat and spotted the young woman coming up the stairs into the department carrying a cardboard drink tray with four coffees in it. He jumped out of his seat and headed for her, signing as he moved to her. *Bristol, it's so good to see you.*

She grinned and handed over the tray of coffees, so

she had her hands free. In the next second, Samantha took the coffee from Julio.

That meant both their hands were free. He held his arms wide, and she slammed into him. Julio gave Samantha's little sister a big hug, then stepped back grinning. *It's been way too long.*

I know, she signed back. *I miss you.* She added her sign for his name on the end.

Julio slung his arm around her and turned her to the room. Romeo still looked like he had been frozen in place.

Julio looked down at Bristol and saw her looking at her sister's partner in a similar way, with a whole lot of pink-cheek shyness. Hence Samantha's reaction to her sister's arrival. She probably realized that Bristol had come here precisely to see Romeo.

"Romeo, come here." He motioned with his head toward Samantha's sister.

The detective slowly walked toward them, but not his usual easy gait. This meant something to him.

At the table, Sam drank her water and didn't look at them. So she didn't want to be involved with this? At least Julio could get over the hitch of introducing them to each other for her.

He turned slightly so Bristol would be able to see his hands and his face. *This is police detective Romeo Alvarez.* He signed each letter one by one, figuring Bristol would come up with her own sign for his name. If their relationship progressed that far.

Maybe Samantha was hoping it wasn't going to.

Far as Julio knew, Romeo was a good guy. If he got the chance, Julio was going to tell her to let them figure it out themselves—although maybe that's what she was doing right now. On the side, he planned to warn Romeo what might happen if he hurt Bristol.

Bristol waived at Romeo, a soft little movement. All nerves and cuteness. Romeo was in serious trouble.

He turned to the guy, but not so far Bristol wouldn't be able to see what he said. He signed, and spoke aloud at the same time, "This is Samantha's sister, Bristol."

Romeo tentatively lifted his hands and signed back, *Hi.*

Okay, then. Apparently, the guy was in the process of doing his homework.

"You can say it out loud as well. She can hear a little if you stand close to her, but not if there's a lot of background noise. She'll learn to read your lips. If you get hung up figuring out how to talk, just exchange numbers and text each other." Julio turned to Bristol, touched her cheeks, and gave her a kiss on the forehead. Then he signed, *Thanks for the coffee.*

She waved him away, and he got the message, going over to where her sister sat. He set one of the drinks in front of Samantha.

She didn't look up. "Is this your doing?"

Julio tugged out a chair and sat beside her, turning to face her so she was his whole focus. "I haven't done anything." He glanced over at Romeo and Bristol, now sitting on two waiting area chairs. He was trying to sign something, and she was adjusting his hands. Both of them were laughing. Romeo pulled out his phone. "You have to admit, it's pretty adorable."

Samantha groaned. "I'm never going to hear the end of this."

Julio didn't think about it, he just lifted his hand and ran it down a strand of her hair. He stopped his hand at the back of her shoulder, caressing with his fingers. Trying to impart some peace into her. Or at least a sense of solidarity. "It'll be okay."

"Unless all goes horribly wrong, and then I'm the one who has to pick up the pieces on both sides. I'll have to see them every day. And they will end up blaming me for the whole disaster."

"But it might not go wrong at all," Julio said. "It just might be very, very right."

She flinched.

Then frowned.

Before he could ask what was going on, she said, "Why is Captain Tennet on TV?"

Julio glanced over. At the bottom of the screen it said his name, scrolling with the words *Arson Investigator*. Then the words *LIVE* and *Breaking News* flashed across the screen. He grabbed the remote from the middle of the table and turned up the volume until he could hear Tennet address the reporters, hands gripping the edges of a podium at a press conference.

"...that we are currently dealing with a copycat of the notorious arsonist Richard Sylvan. We advise the public to go about their lives but do so with caution. It is our belief that this man is extremely dangerous."

THIRTEEN

Even an hour later, Julio was still fuming about the arson investigator's announcement. Samantha could tell, even if he'd finally quit ranting. Not just the fact that Tennet had gone on TV in a press conference without telling anyone else on the task-force, but also because he had announced to the whole city that they were looking for a copycat.

She sat in the passenger seat of his truck, on their way to speak with Richard Sylvana's next of kin. She didn't want to keep rehashing the same thing over and over, but it just wasn't connecting. And it was much better than thinking about her own sister and partner having their first date in the Intelligence bullpen.

Julio was right—it was pretty adorable.

Not that she planned to admit that to *anyone*.

"I just don't understand how Tennet could make that assessment so quickly," she said, glancing over at Julio. "We had barely put it together about the identities of the two victims. He seriously jumped the gun."

"It connects them to Sylvana." He shrugged one shoulder, his movement tight.

"Seems to me like a whole lot of circumstantial evidence when it isn't clear who is doing this or what their motives are." She would never have moved on it in the same situation. "All we did is tip him off to how much information we put together so far."

"Maybe that's the point."

"I don't know how the fire department conducts investigations." She shook her head. "But in the police department, we try not to let the bad guys know that we know what they're doing and that we are onto them. The takedown tends to go better if it's a surprise."

Kind of like the way Bristol had surprised them with coffee. It wasn't until her sister had shown up with four cups instead of three that Samantha realized it was about seeing Romeo. It just so happened that about the same time Romeo decided he wanted to get to know the woman Samantha was having breakfast with at the diner, her sister was also having the same reaction to him. But love at first sight wasn't something Samantha put much stock in.

Was it even a real thing?

And the odds of it happening to both of them at the same time?

It was like watching some kind of bizarre miracle cross with a fairytale unfold in front of her. As if there was still magic in the world, not just death and destruction. Cases. Investigations. Breakups.

She barely knew what to make of it.

Another God-thing?

Samantha said, "I'm thinking maybe I should go to church, or something. Things just seem to be way too confusing and I'm having a hard time understanding what's going on."

Julio reached over and squeezed her hand. "It's a good place to start. I should probably go with you, but..."

She waited for him to say more, but he didn't. "But what?"

"I haven't gone to church in a while. To be honest, I was pretty angry after we broke up."

"After I lost the baby."

He nodded.

"Angry at me?"

"It seemed unfair to be angry at you. Being angry at God was a lot easier, because I knew He could absorb how I felt at the time. When it would have been the wrong thing to lay it on you."

Samantha couldn't help thinking they had dealt with it completely wrong. Even if at the time they both felt that going their separate ways was the right thing. But how could she have done anything else? She'd been in so much pain.

Pushing Julio away had been about self-preservation more than anything else.

Still, she said, "Maybe we were supposed to deal with it alone and then come back together, but we never did. Maybe we missed what we should've done."

They might have missed a whole lot more than that.

But she didn't want to live in all the *could have beens* and *should have beens*. Life just happened that way, and wishing it was otherwise would be pointless. She'd rather deal with reality.

"I think maybe we did miss something," he said. "But we can't say that it was right or wrong at the time. Not when we were both hurting."

Samantha looked out the window, watching buildings pass beside the truck as Julio drove through Benson to the address GPS was directing him. Richard Sylvana's son might prove a fruitful source of intel. Or, at least, she hoped he would.

Or he knew nothing.

Or he might turn out to be their arsonist.

Right now, she had no idea.

She sighed. "Sometimes I feel like everything I want is out of reach. Maybe I did the wrong thing somewhere along the way and missed it. And I lost my shot."

"I don't believe it's ever too late. You and I have been through more than most people do in a lifetime, but that doesn't mean we can't stick through the rest together."

Samantha glanced at him. "But can you guarantee it isn't going to be worse than what we've already been through? Because I don't think I can survive that again."

As far as she could tell, it was safer to stick with what she knew—what she could control.

"I don't have any more answers than you do." Julio sighed. "We can't know what's going to happen. We just have to pledge to stick together through it."

"Because I didn't do that last time? I drove us apart because I couldn't handle what was happening?" Was that what he was saying?

Julio hit the brakes and pulled over to the side of the road. Someone honked, but he ignored it and put the truck in Park. He turned in his seat to face her. "If you want me to blame you, I'm not going to. You had no idea that one shift would put you in a situation where you lost the baby."

Tears gathered in her eyes, the hot sting of regret and grief. "I talked to my sergeant as soon as I showed up for that shift, asking about getting put on desk duty. He was going to put the paperwork through that day." She wouldn't have continued to walk a beat during a pregnancy. But then, she hadn't been super happy about desk duty either. Still, she would never have put the baby's life at risk just so she could do whatever she wanted.

"It was a tragedy that no one could've anticipated would happen. You shouldn't blame yourself, and you should know that I don't blame you."

Maybe it would be better if he did, but that would only mean she could focus on him rather than dealing with her own pain and the need to find some healing. She'd been pushing away her need to deal with it for two years, shutting people out. Focusing on work. Keeping her head down. Pretending she was fine.

She wasn't sure it had worked.

"I don't know what to do." Samantha shifted. "I don't know how to make it not hurt."

"Sometimes I think it's supposed to hurt. Because if you feel nothing, then it means you didn't care."

Tears rolled down her face. So many tears. She'd not only lost the baby, but she'd also lost him. In the blindness of her grief, she'd pushed him away.

Julio reached over and touched her cheeks, swiping at the tears with his thumbs. "You don't need to feel like you're the only one in pain. You aren't alone."

She'd always thought it was easier to just deal with her problems by herself. Maybe that meant she closed herself off to everything and everyone. But it didn't work. And she wasn't sure it had been easier, either.

Even Bristol stayed at arm's length, where Samantha insisted she be. Using the difference of communication to create a wall between them because Samantha didn't want to face her own inability to fix her problem and find some peace. She didn't want to know that Bristol could help her when it was far easier to nurse the hurt.

Because the pain was the only thing she had left.

Julio leaned closer to her, hesitating. Tentative, the way he had always been. But right now, Samantha didn't need him to be gentle with her. She needed someone to break down the wall and force her to share her heart.

She closed the gap between them and pressed her lips to his, pouring all the hurt and grief and longing into that shared moment. Her hands sought him, and she grasped the collar of his shirt, dragging him closer to her. She shifted her fingers to the back of his neck. He didn't tighten his hold on her. Content to allow her to take what she needed from him while he held himself still.

The fact that Julio was being entirely Julio right now was what allowed her to draw back, breathing hard.

The skin around his eyes flexed. "Good?"

She frowned.

"Now it's my turn," he said.

He didn't let her go. He leaned in, still touching her cheeks and pressed his lips to hers. Exquisitely gently, he held her close, and she soaked it in. Drawing deep of all the comfort and connection he wanted to give her.

The churning in her heart and mind eased, softened by the way he settled her like no one else. Like nothing else in her life ever had, or ever would. In a way that made her want to believe that God was real. Because if He wasn't, then all this was nothing but an accident. And she couldn't believe that it could be exactly what she needed, otherwise. There was just no way some random confluence could precisely match her the way that Julio did.

He eased back, and she dipped her head.

Samantha felt his cheek touch hers. She wasn't sure how long it was going to last, but the simple contact was enough to let her feel safe enough to pray.

I'm sorry I didn't believe You.

The simple words in her mind and heart eased more inside Samantha than even Julio's kiss had. She would never have guessed just days ago that she would be here, sitting with him. Feeling like she was actually at peace with God for the first time in a very long time.

And yet she was.

"I could stay here forever."

Julio's voice rumbled close by. "Eventually one of us is going to have to go to the bathroom."

She smiled but didn't move.

"Although, you'll probably need coffee before that happens."

She started to laugh. Then it occurred to her she hadn't done that in a very long time as well. She leaned back, shaking her head. Marveling how much had changed in just a couple of days. It wasn't that she had managed to regain what she lost. Samantha was a much different person than she had been two years ago, and she doubted a relationship between them would be the same.

It wasn't as if everything was fixed.

But at least she was headed in that direction.

The skin around his eyes flexed. "You okay?"

"I am more okay than I've been in a long time." She pushed her hair back, swiping at her cheeks. "And a lot of it is thanks to you."

Julio smiled. "I'm glad I could be here."

"Me, too." She resituated herself in the seat and looked at the screen of her phone. "We should be going."

"Back to reality?" He seemed as reluctant as she was to get back to work.

"Maybe when we clock out at the end of the day, we could go get some dinner or something?" Samantha bit her lip. Why was asking that so awkward? They had eaten together plenty of times. Not to mention everything else that came with creating a life, something neither of them had been proud of—but she knew he would've stuck by her.

By now they would be married with a toddler.

This was just dinner.

He reached over and squeezed her hand. "Sounds good. I know just the place where we can get a good meal."

She wondered where he ate regularly lately and realized again how long it had been since they spent time together. Enough time for him to have found new places and new people.

Meanwhile, she hung out with Bristol and went to work. It had been enough for a long time. But now that Julio was back in her life, it seemed more like a desolate existence.

One she'd have to figure out how to let go.

FOURTEEN

Julio pulled up to the curb in front of the house, feeling better than he had in a long time. He wasn't entirely sure how to process the range of emotions coursing through him. Most of them centered around Samantha and the way she had kissed him. He hoped she understood the difference in his kiss.

Where she had needed to pour out all her frustration, he had wanted to give back peace. Each had found what they needed in that moment.

He hoped they could continue to work things out between them. With all that entailed—plus the part where they went to church together.

Julio put the truck in Park and turned to Samantha. "I know we need to get inside, but I just want to say this."

She looked over at him, her elbows splayed. Using the hair tie from her wrist to secure her blond hair back. Switching from the Samantha he had been making out with, back into Detective Jesse. Exercising a little control where she felt like she didn't have much.

"If we are going to do this again"—he signed *we*—"we should do it differently. We should go to church together."

Samantha nodded, a soft expression on her face. "We do need to get back to work." She grasped the door handle. "But I agree." She got out of the truck, closing the door firmly.

Julio pocketed the keys and followed her up the front walk, glad to see she had bounced back in a way that meant she was going to draw her professionalism around her like a coat and finish the rest of the shift. After that, they could go somewhere quiet and talk. Spend time together.

He'd been thinking about taking her to the firehouse because she hadn't been there in a while. Who knew what they were making for dinner tonight, but it was usually something good and there was always plenty just in case community members dropped in at mealtime. She could see his captain's office, and he could show her his life the way she had shown him hers.

Definitely a lot safer to be in public than in either of their homes and risk their relationship falling back into the old way of doing things.

Samantha knocked on the door, and it started to swing open, creaking. The sound echoed through the house. A single-story structure that didn't look like it had a basement. Probably a crawlspace under the floor. A carport in lieu of a garage, covered with a metal roof that leaned against the right side of the house. Grass on the front lawn that had grown to four or five inches, an ocean of thin stems with tiny flowers on them.

He heard the snick as Samantha drew her weapon from its holster.

She stepped into the house, and he followed her,

staying back. Not because he wanted her to be the one the bullet hit if anything started flying. More like he didn't want to get in the way if she had to defend them both.

"Do I need a gun?" he asked.

"I'll let you know if you do," she replied.

He figured that meant she thought he didn't need one.

"I have a gun at home, in my safe." Not something he usually carried at work, and it was his personal weapon anyway. If there was trouble here, he could quickly dial 9-1-1—which had him pulling out his phone and getting it ready just in case. Samantha might be a cop, but she didn't need to think he wasn't capable of protecting her if it came down to it.

"I don't think you're going to need it today." She hesitated, then stepped into the kitchen. "The smell is usually a lot worse than this."

Julio peered over her shoulder and spotted a man tied to a wooden dining room chair, his hands behind his back. Blood on his chest and face. One of his eyes was almost completely swollen shut. Blood had dripped down the chair to pool on the floor. Not much, but apparently enough that he had succumbed to blood loss.

Samantha circled the room, sticking to the edges. Looking around furniture and out all the windows. "I need to call this in."

"I'll do it." Julio got on the phone with dispatch and moved around the table so he could crouch in front of the man. He explained to the dispatcher who he was and asked for the police. He nearly added a request for the medical examiner, but something caught his eye. "Hold on."

He put the back of his hand in front of the man's

mouth and nose. The faintest hint of breath touched his skin.

"He's alive." Julio patted his cheek. "Mitchell, can you hear me?"

Across the room, Samantha gasped. "How can he possibly be alive? Look at him."

Into the phone, Julio said, "We need an ambulance. Now."

"Dispatching now." The guy on the other end of the phone gave him a three-minute ETA.

Julio hung up even though he wasn't supposed to, and pocketed his phone. "I need something to cut him free, and we need to get pressure on these wounds."

Far as he could see, the guy had been carved up on his chest. Beaten, probably punched. The knife lay on the table—something the police would hopefully be able to use to get fingerprints. Whoever had done this wanted information from the man, surely. Why else torture him?

Julio wondered if the assailant got it and that was why he was gone now.

But he'd left the man alive, instead of leaving him for dead. Which meant when this guy woke up, he would hopefully be able to identify his assailant.

"I have to check out the rest of the house." Samantha handed him a pair of scissors she'd found in a kitchen drawer.

"I've got this." He wanted to squeeze her hand, or kiss her forehead, but there was no time. They were professional enough not to be distracted by personal feelings when a man was dying in the room, and they had a murdering arsonist to find. But the longer the case went on and their feelings continued to be unresolved, the harder it would become.

One kiss hadn't fixed their relationship. But two was a start.

Julio cut the man free and eased him onto the floor. His weight made his lower body drop hard, but Julio braced the guy's upper body with all the strength he had, and then lowered him down. He set the man's head down last, cradling it in his hand. Mitchell didn't need more injuries than he already had.

Julio ran to the front door and pushed it open wide. Then he hit the bathroom and grabbed the towel he found and a stack of rags that were probably washcloths or for cleaning.

The guy kept a decently neat house. He lived minimally, but plenty of people chose to do so. Not much as far as personal effects scattered around the house. The file Samantha had put together that they'd read over before they left indicated he worked for a local tech company in a cubicle, coding or doing some kind of programming.

Not something Julio understood. All he'd ever done was fight fires.

The idea of working in a tiny box and doing the same thing every day, typing away on a computer, sounded like his idea of a nightmare. He much preferred to be active. When his duties became rote, he'd done the work to form a bomb squad with two other firefighters, two police officers, and one of the EMTs in Benson.

One day the mayor would sign off on the team as legit and they would receive more than minimal funding. But it hadn't happened yet.

One day...

Right now, the future looked a whole lot brighter than it had even just this morning.

"Captain Coda!" The man's yell echoed down the hallway.

"Kitchen!" Julio called back.

The EMTs raced into the room a few seconds later, carrying duffel bags and pushing a stretcher down the hall with them. "What have we got?"

Julio pressed the towel against the man's chest wounds. "Mitchell Sylvana. Thirty-two-year-old male. Multiple stab wounds to his chest. Bruising, contusions, and swelling on his face. The side of his ribs looks nasty as well. His pulse is low, and his breathing is very shallow."

He was pretty sure that covered all they needed to know, but he probably missed something. It had been a while since he used any of the EMT training the department required all the firefighters to have. Being a captain meant he didn't go on many routine calls.

If he were honest, he did miss it. Not just because he did a lot more paperwork these days.

"We've got it from here."

"Copy that." Julio rocked back on his heels and straightened out of his crouch while the EMTs took over assessing the guy. They would lift him onto the stretcher and wheel him out as fast as they could, rushing him to the hospital so he could be treated. But the first job would be stabilizing him.

In the hopes he'd make it to the hospital alive.

Julio was pretty sure they were looking at the arsonist as the main suspect for who had done this. However, despite Tennet's press conference, the taskforce still had no idea who that might be. Even with the FBI looking at the letters Richard Sylvana had received, all they really had was a personality profile. And unless the suspect made himself known, how were they going to find him?

The press conference announcing him as a copycat had probably been a long shot, and Captain Tennet likely knew they would all disagree with his decision to go ahead with it. Probably why he never told them.

Julio didn't like being blindsided much more than he liked being left out of decisions made concerning a team he was part of.

Was Samantha right that it would either tip off the suspect to the fact they were looking for him, or maybe send him on a rampage out of anger? No matter what came of the press conference announcement, it was already done. All they could do was deal with the fallout.

He and Samantha knew well enough that the past wasn't something they were able to change. Considering the moment they'd had in the truck, he figured she was onboard with him and looking to the future.

Maybe being more successful this time around.

He wandered through the house, looking for Samantha. She was probably doing her police detective assessment of the man's things. Out the living room window, he saw a black-and-white police car pull up.

Romeo had gone to interview the employees from the warehouse, so it wouldn't be him unless he'd heard Julio's call to dispatch and was able to get away.

Julio checked in empty room, with one single cardboard box in the corner. Next down the hall was the bathroom, also empty. He went to the bedroom because it was the last place to look.

But Samantha wasn't in here.

He frowned, turning in a circle. Pulled out his phone and called her number, listening to it ring while he checked the closet. It was the only other space he hadn't looked in, the single bathroom being in the hallway. She didn't answer.

"Where did you go?"

No one answered his muttered question. The call switched to voicemail, and he heard her tell him to leave a message after the beep.

Julio hung up and opened his messages. He found Bristol in his contacts and sent her a text.

> Can you look up Samantha's location on your phone?

He wandered through the house back to the front door, figuring she was likely out there if she wasn't inside the house. Or was she in the backyard? Maybe she had seen something and gone outside.

The two uniformed officers walked up the front path toward the door.

Julio said, "Have you seen Detective Jesse out here?"

Both shook their heads. His phone buzzed, so he looked down at the screen. Bristol had sent him a screenshot of a map with Samantha's GPS location. Not entirely accurate usually, so he wasn't sure how far he could trust it. But Samantha seemed to be two streets away.

What was going on?

FIFTEEN

Samantha raced along the sidewalk, her gun drawn, sticking to as many spots where she could find cover as possible. Up ahead, a lone man walked swiftly along the sidewalk. His shoes clipped the concrete.

He never once turned back, but she didn't trust that her own steps were silent. She had no clue if he was aware of her behind him.

She'd seen him outside at the end of the backyard. Staring at the house from the other side of a chain-link fence. She wasn't sure she could have articulated what it was about him that had her rushing through the house and leaving the front door with only a callout to Julio that she wasn't sure he'd heard.

Did some part of her subconscious remember him?

The EMTs had been pulling down the street at the same time. Julio had help. She could take care of herself. So she'd raced out after this guy.

Just in case.

The man turned down a side street, probably headed

for his car or another residence nearby. Was he out walking and he'd seen commotion in the arsonist's son's house? Just some kind of interested bystander with no connection? Mitchell Sylvana had never changed his last name, unlike his grandmother. The question was, why had it taken the arsonist longer to find him? At least, that's who she was banking on had attacked Mitchell in his home.

But why tie him to a chair and interrogate him?

What was he hoping to gain from asking Mitchell questions he didn't want to answer?

She had enough faith to pray Mitchell woke up in the hospital and was able to give them a full statement. Enough to ask for Julio to be safe at the house right now and for herself, that she wouldn't run headlong into danger.

Samantha stopped at the closest front yard, where another street intersected with this one. She moved across the grass to the corner of the house and peered around the siding, sticking to cover.

This side street led to downtown, but that was still half a mile down. An older part of town that had been here far longer than the bustling high-rises in the center of Benson. Once the main part of the city, these buildings were older with historical markers on them. Brown brick structures that might have been standing for a hundred years.

She couldn't see the man ahead of her.

Samantha crept out from behind the house and hurried down the sidewalk. He might have gone into another building or ducked out of sight, where he was now waiting.

She kept her phone in one hand, her gun in the other,

taking measured steps. Her heart pounding in her ears, her eyes scanning the streets, buildings, and anywhere she could see. Everything in her was hyperaware of what was happening around her.

Which meant she heard the shuffle as soon as it happened.

Samantha spun back, rotating on the ball of her foot so that her shoe scraped gravel as she turned. He grabbed for the gun. She tightened her grip, punching forward with her phone hand to slam into the guy's sternum.

Breath expelled from his lips, hot and sour.

She pulled back far enough to lift her foot and kicked at him. His grip on her gun didn't loosen, dragging her as he stumbled back a couple of steps. She planted her feet, but he pulled her over and rolled, coming up on top of her. The gun skittered out of reach.

Samantha only had her phone, which she slammed up toward the guy's face. It smashed into his cheek and nose, and she heard the satisfying crack of cartilage.

He cried out, and blood sprayed her shoulder.

She gritted her teeth.

His hands grasped at her neck, banding around her throat where he started to squeeze. Blood stained his teeth, and he breathed hard. Not quite panic but certainly amped up because she had proven more formidable than he expected.

Black spots flickered at the edges of her vision.

She grabbed at his hands around her throat, trying to pry them away from the death grip that felt as if it were crushing her windpipe.

She batted at his arms and pushed at his shoulders. But no matter what she tried, there was no way to push him off her.

Lord, help me.

Her strength began to wane. She could feel the energy she had as if it seeped from her into the ground underneath her. She wanted to study his features to memorize them. But if she was about to lose her life here and now, what would be the point?

He knew she had seen his face. Now, she was going to die.

With her last morsel of strength, Samantha pushed at him. She kicked her legs, but couldn't dislodge him.

A thunder of steps crested the edge of her awareness, growing in volume. "Sammy!"

That was when she knew she was going to die. The only time Julio ever called her that was in the worst moments. The times when it was nearly over.

Julio slammed into the man, tackling him to the side.

Samantha tried to breathe. She fought to inhale, managing only a tiny bit of air.

What was he...

How were they...

She turned her head far enough she could see what was going on.

Julio punched the man in the face, whipping his head to the side. The guy cried out, and Julio flipped him onto his stomach. "I need something to secure him with!"

Samantha had cuffs on the back of her belt.

She closed her eyes and slowly inhaled through her nose, drawing in as much clean air as possible. She lifted her hip just enough to slide her hand to the small of her back and tugged out the cuffs, sending them skittering across the ground.

Which was when she remembered her gun had done the same thing.

Where was it now?

She heard the clink of metal as Julio secured the man, then the thunderous sound of him yelling into his phone. Calling for the police and an ambulance.

And then everything went black.

Samantha awoke to the overly warm sensation of heavy blankets, secured tightly around her. She had an oxygen mask over her nose, tucked behind her head. No one had pulled the hair tie from her ponytail, so the tight material securing her hair back dug into the back of her scalp. She shifted her head from side to side, trying to alleviate the discomfort.

Someone touched her hand. "Hey."

She managed to curl her fingers into his, though there was little strength in her grip. With some effort, she managed to blink her eyes open, and Julio came into focus beside the bed. Sitting in a chair with his arm outstretched so he could hold her hand.

He smiled. "There you are."

She swallowed, which hurt a lot. But she managed to say, "Thanks to you." The sound of her voice low, and broken. She then tugged her hand away from his and signed, *What is going on?*

Julio sat with his forearms on his knees. "Some cops came and took that guy away. I went with you in the ambulance, but I called your sergeant and filled her in on what happened. You were out for a couple of hours, so the doctors did their full assessment. I should tell them that you're awake."

She shook her head. *Who was that guy?*

"Sergeant Deerdan was trying to figure it out the last I spoke to her. She called me about fifteen minutes ago and said they had him booked in and they were trying to work out who he was. If he's the arsonist, then we're done because he's in custody and he won't be getting out anytime soon."

Samantha wasn't entirely sure it would be that simple.

"And if he isn't, then someone else dangerous is off the streets." He looked at his phone. "Bristol is on her way up."

Samantha nodded. Her sister was probably frantically rushing from the elevator, and Samantha didn't blame her. If anything happened to Bristol, she would react the same way. She signed, *Don't tell her he tried to choke the life out of me.*

Julio winced. "With the bruising on your throat, it might be a little obvious that something serious happened. I'm not going to tell her you tripped."

She pulled the oxygen mask off. "Tell her you arrested the guy. Distract her with your heroics." She coughed a little.

Julio got a water cup from the side table and held the straw to her lips. She spotted her gun and her badge beside the bed—where she knew it had been placed in order to help her feel secure. Her things were safe, not in the wrong hands. She might be injured, but she was still a cop.

The ice-cold water didn't feel good at first, but she drank enough to numb her throat.

Julio said, "I should get you some tea."

She stared at him. How long had it been since he had made tea for her? She couldn't even remember, but he drank it often and she usually asked for one as well. Though, with a little sugar in it.

She wondered then if maybe she only drank coffee so much because tea just didn't taste the same when Julio hadn't made it for her.

He squeezed her foot through the blankets. "I'll get you some tea."

And just like that, all the topsy-turvy equilibrium she felt had righted itself, as if everything had clicked back into place. All that had been nothing but dissonant fragments for the last two years moved to where they should be. In perfect alignment.

"Oh, here you go." He handed over her phone, the screen almost completely cracked.

Julio left the door open, and while he was gone, she sent a text message to her sergeant, telling her she was awake and asking who the man was that had attacked her. Then she sent an update to Romeo, not sure what he knew.

Had they really arrested the arsonist?

It would be a good thing if they had. It might even make the pain in her throat worth it, and all the days being irritated that it hurt—right up until it healed. If they hadn't, they'd logged the arrest of a dangerous man at least. One who could have killed her or potentially others as well if Julio hadn't got there in time to save her.

A rap on the door drew her attention. Bristol might not totally be able to hear the knock she made on the wood, but she understood how the hearing world announced their arrival.

Samantha glanced over. Behind Bristol, Romeo appeared.

Samantha's eyes narrowed. Had they arrived at the

same time, or had they been together? Romeo was supposed to have been working.

Bristol came over and gave Samantha a hug, her hands a flurry of questions and concerns. Samantha waited until she was finished, and then told her she was fine.

Bristol gave her the most *yeah right* look Samantha had ever seen on her sister's face. But at least they understood each other well enough that Bristol slumped into the chair and thankfully looked less worried than she had when she first came into the room.

Romeo watched from the door, a look of curious amusement on his face. "I might have no idea what you're saying to each other, but I get the gist from your facial expressions. My sister looks at me like that sometimes as well. Like I exasperate her."

Samantha managed to smile, interpreting what he'd said for her sister. Then she said, "I want to know who this guy is."

Romeo smiled softly at Bristol while Samantha said that, and then said, "I'll call Deerdan and find out." He tugged out his phone and stepped into the hallway.

Samantha turned her head back toward her sister, nudging her ponytail.

Bristol got up and tapped her shoulder, getting Samantha to lean forward so she could pull the hair tie out. Samantha shook her head and signed, *Thanks.*

Bristol wasn't happy. *This case is going to kill you.*

"You don't know that." Samantha signed as she spoke. "Neither do I."

The exasperated look returned to her sister's face.

SIXTEEN

J ulio headed down the hospital hallway, toward the room where the nurse had told him he might find Mitchell Sylvana. He'd run out and grabbed a sandwich, checked in with the firehouse, and come back. But before he went to Samantha's room, he wanted to check on the arsonist's son.

The nurse hadn't been able to give him any information about the guy's condition, which wasn't surprising given HIPAA regulations. However, the fact that he was in a room and not in the morgue told him enough information about whether or not they'd succeeded in saving his life.

Julio still couldn't shake the image of finding Samantha on the ground, that guy on top of her.

If it hadn't been for Bristol and her ability to locate Samantha's phone, he might never have found her. She could have been choked to death on the street and he'd have had no idea.

Until it was too late.

His hands shook. Abrasions and bruising covered his

knuckles where he'd slammed his fist into that guy. Julio probably would've kept going long enough to kill the guy —or at least do some serious damage—if it wasn't for the fact that Samantha had been watching.

They needed to know if he was the arsonist.

Something they might not have been able to find out if Julio had killed him.

She should get credit for the arrest, and things would not be messed up because of him. At least as far as he could control things. Which, given she nearly died, might not be too much. Although the anger in him had subsided some, he wasn't exactly ready to jump back in with both feet and claim to be a Christian again.

He might have lived a quiet life for the last two years, but his actions before that didn't exactly spell out the kind of person who followed the Bible.

Julio stopped outside the room, turning so he could lean back against the wall. The most he could say was a quiet thank-you to God for getting him there in time. For the fact she was still alive right now, even if they weren't entirely out of the woods. He didn't think the doctors would keep her overnight, but someone needed to monitor her condition. Swelling in the throat could have nasty consequences.

His own throat closed reflexively. He swallowed against it and knocked on the door.

He heard a quiet, "Come in," but it wasn't a male voice.

Julio turned the handle and stayed by the doorway. She sat in a chair beside the bed, dark hair that had been dyed and a heavy metal band T-shirt. She had a pale face and dark-red lips.

The man in the bed lay tucked under the sheets,

bandages on the areas of his skin that were visible. Tubes had been placed across his face with little notches in his nostrils, adding a clean air mix to what he breathed.

"I'm Captain Julio Espinoza-Vasquez from the fire department. I'm working on an arson investigation task-force, and I was with the detective when we found Mr. Sylvana."

"You're one of the ones?" She sat up a little straighter, her voice low and graveled. "I'm Terri."

"That's right, my partner is a police detective and we'd come to talk to Mitchell. I'm just glad that we found him in time."

Her shoulders tensed. "Talk to him about what?"

"Is Mitchell a friend of yours?" Julio asked. "Or a boyfriend?"

Dodging his question, she said, "Is he being suspected of those fires, like the ones his father set?"

"He isn't one of our suspects." At least, he wasn't once they had stepped inside the house and found him. "We only wanted to see if he could shed any light on the situation."

"He didn't have anything to do with it."

Julio studied her. "What makes you so sure of that?"

Maybe she didn't know him as well as she thought she did. Probably the police would want to question her and Mitchell when he awoke, but there was no reason why he couldn't establish a rapport between her and the arson investigation taskforce.

"He hates his father and everything he did. But his mom ditched when his dad got arrested, so he wound up in a foster home. Same one as me."

Julio frowned. "His grandmother didn't offer to take him in?"

The woman looked confused. "What grandmother?"

He wasn't sure he wanted to explain that she was the first victim of this current arsonist. "She changed her name, so maybe she wanted nothing to do with the family. Seems like Mitchell may not have been so lucky."

Not that what had happened to either of them—Mitchell and his grandmother—could be considered good fortune.

"He didn't even want to talk about the fires, or his parents." She shook her head. "The kids at school never left him alone for one second through the trial and after. Our school was miserable for him, but we stuck together. We've been friends ever since."

"I'm sure he's very grateful to have someone like you in his life."

Julio's existence the past two years had been pretty solitary, even though he'd taken a couple of trips to see his parents. It wasn't like he had a ton of people who would show up to his hospital room if he were here, hurt. Even just one who cared enough to be the only person that showed up—like Terri with Mitchell, or he and Bristol with Samantha.

Who would've shown up for him?

Until recently, not even Samantha would have. Although, he had never removed her as his next of kin.

If something happened to him on the job, the entire waiting room would be full of firefighters. But that was about standing with a brother who had been hurt putting his life on the line. It didn't matter who it was. Everyone turned out.

To him, it almost had more meaning when a single person would sit by a hospital bedside.

"Do you have any idea why someone might want to

hurt Mitchell?" It had almost seemed as if they were interrogating him, or at the least punishing him for something. Whether it was about gaining information or not.

"He keeps his head down. He doesn't bother anyone, and he expects people not to bother him." She shrugged one shoulder. "Sometimes they do, but when the police figure out who he is, they don't seem to be interested in stopping the harassment."

Julio wasn't a cop, so he couldn't speak to that. But he didn't think it was appropriate for the police to do that. He should ask Samantha to look up Mitchell in the PD reports. "Anyone in particular you can think of lately? Someone who might want to hurt him?"

"Not really." She brushed her hair back. "But he doesn't always tell me about it. Since there's nothing either of us can do."

"Thank you for talking to me." He pulled a business card from his wallet. "If you think of anything, or if you and Mitchell need any help, feel free to call me or anyone at my firehouse."

She blinked at the card, then looked at him. "Thanks."

Julio stepped back out into the hallway and made his way back to Samantha's room. She had the door closed, so he repeated the same knock he'd done with Mitchell's room.

"One second."

He eased his stance over and leaned on the doorframe.

When the door finally opened, Samantha stood there. Pale skin, and dark circles under her eyes. They didn't match the bruising around her neck, but she still needed rest.

She had changed into black leggings and a comfort-able-looking T-shirt, a sweater pulled over her shoulders and now hanging down by her sides even though it was warm out. On her feet she had a pair of flat canvas shoes. She looked a lot like the girl he had known, once upon a time. Not so much like the tough-as-nails police detective he had been working with.

Truth be told, he liked both sides of her. The strong and the vulnerable. The way she knew how to accept help at the right time, and also how to stand up for herself when needed.

But the best part of who she was would always be the way she stood up for other people.

Julio glanced around. "Did Bristol take off?"

"Romeo was hungry, so I told them to get something to eat and go home. I figured when you came back, I could ask you for a ride."

"Good call." He absolutely wanted to be the one to drive her back to her house. "You have everything?"

"Except a clean bill of health, but that's a problem for tomorrow-Samantha. Today-Samantha is interested in getting where she's going so she can sit with her eyes closed and try to figure out how to eat pizza with a sore throat." She handed him some papers and a plastic sack.

Julio chuckled. "How about soup?"

"Depends what kind of soup it is."

"We could run by the store on the way to your house and pick something up?"

She scrunched up her face. "I probably have some-thing in the cupboard like chicken noodle or tomato that we haven't eaten yet."

"We?"

"Bristol and I have been roommates since..."

Julio reached out and snagged her hand, curling his fingers around hers. Just a little measure of solidarity, but it was enough for right now. "That's good."

"How about you? Do you live with anyone?"

"Just me."

He often rattled around in that empty house, wondering if he should get a dog and then dismissing the idea because he was at the firehouse way too much. One of the guys at work already had a dog he brought with him to be their mascot. She liked to chew the pillows on the couch when they were out on calls and had pooped in the women's bathroom at least twice.

"So, anyway..." Samantha began but didn't finish.

Yeah, he hadn't explained where he lived. Or what kind of place it was. As soon as he did, she would realize far too much.

"Soup and some soft bread," Julio said. "Maybe a soggy cheese sandwich that's all gooey."

"That sounds terrible and intriguing at the same time."

"You are really good to get out of here?" He hit the button for the elevator either way.

She nodded. "Because of you."

Julio tugged her over and wound his arms around her, giving her a supportive hug. It occurred to him that when it all shook out, this might be all she was prepared to give him. That they might be forever destined to remain friends. Never more than that, because of their shared history.

All the pain they'd been through might eclipse anything good they could have, like flying too close to the sun. No matter if you were happy, you'd still burn up.

But was it worth a shot at survival? At the chance for something good on the other end?

When the orderly came over with a wheelchair, she flashed her badge at him. The guy backed away. Julio walked her to the lobby and had her sit while he retrieved his truck. When he parked at the curb out front, she came out. Walking slowly enough, he hopped out and went around to the passenger side, pulled the door open for her, and held her hand while she climbed in.

When he got in the driver's side, she had already entered her address in the GPS.

He knew that side of town, not under the purview of his firehouse. Probably on purpose, in case of a fire. Two lives running side by side but never intersecting.

Until a few days ago.

"Wake me when we get there."

She had to feel terrible if she was willing to let down her guard enough to go to sleep while he drove. Julio kept the music low, taking an easy route to her house and wondering as he did if this was all part of some bigger plan for them to restart their relationship.

And all he needed to do was yield to it.

SEVENTEEN

As Samantha swallowed some of the soup, she eyed Julio. "What did you do to it?"

He stood in her kitchen, rinsing a pot in the sink. He glanced over his shoulder, far too good-looking to be doing dishes in any woman's kitchen. Let alone hers. That perennial soft spot she'd always had for him was a sucker for those shoulders in that fire department uniform and the fact he insisted on rinsing dishes before putting them in the dishwasher.

"You don't like it?" he said.

"It's chicken noodle soup. Who doesn't like chicken noodle soup? I'm just asking why it tastes different than it normally does."

He wiped his hands on a kitchen towel. Shrugged. "I added some seasoning."

She wasn't going to let go of the suspicion that he was keeping a secret. Even if it was only how to make chicken noodle soup taste better than when it came out of the can.

Her phone buzzed on the breakfast bar. She flipped it

over far enough to see the screen. "Bristol wants to know if we have any popcorn."

Julio leaned his hips back against the cupboard across from her, the breakfast bar between them. Where it should have felt like there was far too much space between them, it was more like this room didn't seem big enough. No surprise in her tiny apartment that she shared with her sister, but it was more cozy than anything. Who knew what it would feel like when he came and sat beside her.

Was he going to do that?

"Do you have any?" Julio said. "I can nuke it for you guys."

"She can come out and get it herself. She's curled up next to Romeo on the couch in her room." She rolled her eyes. "Watching a movie. As if I don't know what that means."

Julio grinned. "I'm pretty sure it just means they are watching a movie. What do you think it means when they literally just talked for the first time today?"

"Who knows what the kids are doing these days? Or what they're calling it."

He chuckled a little. "Eat your soup. I'll see if there's any popcorn in the pantry."

She shoved a bite from the spoon in her mouth, watching him discover that there was in fact no pantry. The folding doors on one side disguised the washer and dryer, and other than that, she only had cupboards and a refrigerator.

Maybe he was disappointed in her existence. She had been squirreling money away for a long time, saving for a down payment on a house. The house she wanted more than anything. Something out of the way and secluded.

When she purchased the property, she would be able to carve out her own sanctuary from the world. A spot where she could go to rest and feel as if she didn't have to worry about criminals or victims. A place of respite from the world.

"Oh, found it." He grabbed a popcorn package out of the box. "Last one."

"I'll text Bristol back. Tell her to come and get it herself."

He peeled off the plastic wrapper and put the bag in the microwave. It was a test of a person's sanity, and their intelligence, as to whether they use the popcorn button or not. Thankfully for his sake, he passed the test and simply entered a series of numbers.

Samantha ate her soup quietly, enjoying the soothing feeling of warm liquid on her throat. Grateful for the ability to have sustenance even if she couldn't eat most things right now. The doctor had told her that her throat could increase in swelling at any time, and she needed to be very careful not to irritate it.

Bristol had told the doctor that she would keep an eye on Samantha. Something she was currently *not* doing. Samantha had interpreted for the doctor so he could understand what her sister was saying, and then her sister promptly ditched Samantha for a guy as soon as they got home. Probably because she thought it would give Samantha and Julio time to spend together.

Maybe Romeo was in on it as well.

Samantha wasn't entirely disappointed in them. As long as Julio didn't know he was being hoodwinked. It was embarrassing enough that her partner was probably in on the plan, given all the texting Bristol had been doing.

The truth was, she did want to spend time with Julio. Getting to know him again the last few days—reacquainting herself with the man he was now—had given her a sense of hope she hadn't had before. Not for a long time.

Julio had been the best thing in her life. But like all good things, they inevitably turned bad, and she had to manage the fallout. The bad with him had been epically bad, given the miscarriage she'd had after being thrown out of that building. The grief. Their breakup. She wasn't sure she would be able to handle going through all that again, but something in her wanted to try.

Julio pulled out the popcorn. He turned and pointed at the hall. "That way?"

He had a very "big brother" expression on his face, which was good because who knew what moves Romeo had made on her sister. She knew how Julio felt about Bristol. In fact, she'd always loved the way he looked out for her sister just like she did.

"Last door on the right." As she spoke, her phone rang.

He squeezed her shoulder and wandered away.

She looked at the screen and saw it was Sergeant Deerdan calling. "Jesse." Her voice came out hoarse.

"You sound a lot better than I thought you would," her boss said.

"Any update on the guy we arrested?" She hadn't heard anything from Romeo while she was in the hospital. Samantha had resigned herself to the fact she wouldn't get to listen in on the interrogation, let alone actually be there participating. But she still wanted to know what happened with the man they'd arrested.

"That's why I'm calling," Deerdan said. "We ran his

ID, and his name is Bill Morrison. He's a local guy, but we can't find any employment or a last known address. I have units going to the address associated with this driver's license. The whole thing is looking pretty thin, but maybe he's just a guy who lives small."

"What did he say about attacking me?"

Deerdan made humming sound in her throat. "Well, that's the thing. He claims he actually thought you were attacking *him*. That he was acting in self-defense."

"Did he lawyer up?"

"No, he declined representation."

Samantha figured it was likely that he believed he knew exactly what he was doing and had the whole thing in hand—or he believed he did. "He really claims I attacked him first?"

"You need to write down your statement and get it to us. Morrison will be arraigned in the morning, probably before lunch. We need to know your side of things if we're going to have any way of keeping him in jail long enough to tie him to the fires."

And the murders.

"I'll get that typed up tonight," Samantha said. "Then email it to you."

"I'll be here." Deerdan made another noise. "Dumb coffee pot," she muttered. Then she said, "He actually claims that you were following him for a number of blocks. He was only out walking. Then when he tried to ask you why you were following him, you launched yourself at him and he tried to de-escalate the situation."

She laughed out loud, a barking sound that dissolved into a whole lot of coughing.

Julio jogged quickly down the hallway, concern on his face.

She waved off his concern, signing, *I'm fine.* But he obviously didn't agree with that assessment because he got her a glass of water.

"I also need a statement from Captain Coda," Deerdan added.

Samantha glanced at Julio, accepting the water. "He can do that." Then had to ask, "Do you think we can get enough evidence to tie him to the arsons?" She set the phone on the counter and hit the Speaker button.

Deerdan's voice came through loud enough for Julio to hear as well. "Right now, we have no evidence that he is our arsonist."

Samantha couldn't even confirm it either. All she could do was go with her gut. That creepy guy had been looking across the yard into the window, and she'd felt compelled to chase after him.

Her boss continued, "He may have engaged with you for a bunch of different reasons. None of which he's inclined to explain to us."

Samantha tapped a finger on the counter. "He's probably goading us, knowing we have nothing to arrest him on. He's going to walk free, satisfied that he has all the power here."

"If he does, I'm sure I don't have to explain to you that you *cannot* approach him. I'll have uniformed officers watching him at all times, which will likely just guarantee he doesn't slip up. No way he'll set another fire now. However, there's nothing you can do about it. Don't try and incriminate him. Understood?"

Julio frowned.

Samantha shrugged. "Yes, I understand, Sergeant."

"Good. Don't let a lowlife like this ruin a perfectly good and very promising career." Deerdan paused. "One day you're going to sit in my chair, and any misstep in this case will ruin that chance. Don't flush it all down the toilet."

The call ended.

"I guess that's it." Samantha looked at Julio, still frowning. "What are you thinking? Because we can talk about it, but then we both have homework."

That didn't make him smile. Instead, he scratched his jaw. "She really thinks you're going to do something to incriminate the guy?"

"I thought you were more worried about the fact he'll probably be released tomorrow." Samantha paused. "Unless we can find evidence that ties into this case."

"He's totally messing with us. That whole thing was a setup," Julio said. "Just a way to prove to us how little we know about him by dangling himself in front of us and even getting arrested."

"Arson is about power, isn't it?"

"Power over material things. Over life and death, even." Julio winced. "Maybe she is right that we shouldn't go anywhere near him. But I don't want to be taken off this case."

"Me either, which is why we're going to do our jobs. We won't let him get under our skin, no matter how much he tries to get us to screw this whole thing up."

One wrong thing, and the whole case could be thrown out during the trial. Even the right thing could get a whole case thrown out.

Sometimes there was nothing a cop could do, even if they knew someone was guilty as sin. Without admissible evidence, the person may as well be innocent.

"I'm down for that if you are," Julio said. "We let it go and do what we can." He set his elbows on the breakfast bar across from her, leaning down to level his face with hers. "What do you say?"

"We work this together," Samantha agreed. "And we do it smart." But why did she get the feeling they were talking about more than just the case?

"No matter what ideas Captain Tennet has about how to resolve the situation," he muttered, as though he was still mad about the press conference.

"No matter how much I want to slap Romeo up the backside of the head," she added.

Julio grinned. "He was sitting a reasonable distance from her. They're watching some funny movie from the nineties I can't remember the name of, and they both seem to be enjoying themselves."

She frowned. "Fine."

Julio took her bowl to the sink. "Grudging acceptance is the first step to being onboard with it."

"Great. I'm looking forward to the part where I catch them making out."

Julio tipped his head back and laughed. "Two can play that game. If they're going to do it to you, then maybe you should try and beat them at their own tactics."

Maybe it wasn't going to be that bad, Bristol and Romeo. She did like the idea of her sister being happy with a guy. Samantha just wasn't sure how she felt about it being a guy she worked with. Someone who had no connections to the deaf community.

But considering her track record of successful relationships, maybe she should let them make their own happiness.

And she would try to find some for herself.

With a good man she'd always loved.

EIGHTEEN

To whom it may concern.

Richard hammered on the backspace key rather than holding it down. That wasn't going to be how he started this letter.

This manifesto.

They had made this personal, and now he would do the same.

A little kid collided with the edge of the table, sticky fingers, and a wet stain on his T-shirt. Richard stared at the thing.

"Sorry." A rotund woman with a matching stain on her T-shirt grabbed the kid's arm. "Come on, Leland."

He watched them head into the children's section of the library, the kid racing ahead until it tripped and promptly erupted into wailing. Richard stared as the mother yanked him up and they disappeared into the stacks. The wailing echoed through the library.

He turned back to the computer and searched through the police department's website long enough to ascertain the format for Benson PD officer emails.

Samantha Jesse was a ridiculous name, so it was unlikely there was more than one to be found in a midsize department like the one in this city.

He addressed the email to her.

By now you may believe you know who I am.

Some have called me a copycat. A replica. A wannabe.

I assure you that I am none of these things. I am a student, I am the teacher. One day the truth of what I aim to accomplish will be fully realized. I will have completed the work I set out to do, and I will disappear forever, never to be seen again.

You will not stop me. Just as the fire consumes its fuel, so I will be consumed.

The work that was begun with Richard Sylvana shall be completed. I will bring his dream to fruition, and yet more...

One day soon I will transform. I will become the master and finally what I am meant to be. I will ascend beyond heights Sylvana never realized. Able to go beyond the meager beginning he achieved before he failed.

There will be no such failure for me.

My heart is pure. My intentions will be realized, the final steps irrevocable. The end. A new beginning. The start of something else rising from the ashes of what never should have been.

We will meet again, Detective.

One day soon.

RICHARD READ IT OVER TWICE, MADE A COUPLE OF corrections and then hit Send. He sat back in the chair, now aware of the quiet drone of humanity, life forced to mute itself to adhere to the strictures of this building. The same way the police, the fire department, would have to bend to his will.

He wouldn't be stopped, no matter how hard they tried.

A small chuckle slipped from his mouth. He swallowed it back down. They thought they were so clever, but he would forever be smarter than each of them. As much as this sorry excuse they called a taskforce tried, they might as well admit failure. Inevitably, they would fall far short.

He logged off the computer—and whoever had left their library account signed in.

Richard used the facilities on the way out. Then walked outside, past the bike rack, and glanced back at the gentleman smoking a cigarette there. "Those things'll kill ya."

A chuckle was the only accompaniment he had to the curb, then the step off. A walk to the car.

He climbed in, enjoying for a moment the stifling heat of the interior. Before the air-conditioning pumped enough cool air through the vents to break the heat.

Soon enough, it would consume everything, even him. But there would be no rush. Richard would ensure all the pieces were in place, the setup so flawless it would be executed perfectly. Destruction. Cleansing. All of it would be the ultimate statement, and he would be at the center of it all.

Reborn.

The only way to continue to the next stage of his life was to complete the mission here on earth. To finally wash away all the sin he had removed with the sizzle and curl of flames. Heat that purified the heart of man, consuming all that did not deserve to remain.

Leaving only holiness.

Richard parked and threaded through the lot to the rear entrance of the building. The meeting had already started, but his usual spot in the back row remained empty.

Up at the front of the room, a banner hung from the ceiling behind the altar. The cross, that instrument of torture, flames of fire on either side. Orange and red fabrics, sewn around the symbol of new life. Laced with gold thread so that it flickered and danced the way that flames did.

He had known the first time he saw it that he believed.

Reverend Jameson read from the Good Book, a huge ceremonial tome that took up the whole pulpit. He took a deep breath and said, "Yet once more I shake not the earth only, but also heaven. And this word, Yet once more, signifieth the removing of those things that are shaken, as of things that are made, that those things which cannot be shaken may remain. Wherefore we receiving a kingdom which cannot be moved, let us have grace, whereby we may serve God acceptably with reverence and godly fear."

Richard knew these words. He had hidden these things in his heart, but one day soon all would be revealed. The will of God on earth would be realized.

The final verse he spoke aloud, along with the pastor and everyone else in the room.

"For our God is a consuming fire."

NINETEEN

Julio closed the door of his work truck and walked from the engine bay to the entrance that led into the firehouse, his jacket in one hand. Gripping the material tight gave him something tactile to focus on—something outside of his mind and the images still swirling there.

"I'm gonna hit the showers." The lieutenant of his Rescue Squad slapped Julio on the back shoulder and turned down a different hall.

Julio nodded and continued toward his office.

The others filtered in behind him, headed for the locker room or the kitchen. Even if they still had blood on them, some of the guys insisted on coffee first. They would take it into the showers with them and leave it on the floor just outside the curtain. A hot drink that was more like a lifeline sometimes.

As he wandered down the hallway, the building intercom chimed. "Captain Coda to the Chief's office ASAP."

Julio pushed open the door to his tiny captain's office

and tossed the jacket on his cot. Then he turned on his heel and jogged through to the other wing of the building and upstairs to the offices.

Chief Frayer's assistant sat behind her desk, red-rimmed glasses perched on her nose as she typed. Her long nails clacked on the keyboard.

Julio spotted Greyson through the window, currently on the phone. He grabbed a chair from another desk, currently unoccupied, and tugged it over to the short side of Viola's desk. He set his elbows on a clear spot. "Good morning, Vi. How are you today?"

She didn't look over, but her features took on a pinched expression. "Too busy to be interrupted, even by a cutie such as yourself," she replied, still typing.

Julio chuckled. "Maybe you should have sat in on that sexual harassment seminar with us last month."

She made a face. "I'm going to tell Reginald you said that." She chuckled lightly. "He'll get a kick out of the insinuation I'm some kind of hussy."

Julio prepared himself for another one of her "in my heyday" stories. These days, she was helping Ashlyn and Greyson plan their wedding, and she and Reginald were about to have their second grandchild within the next couple of months.

She finished typing and looked at him. "Did you need something?"

Apparently, he had skated out of listening to a story he'd probably heard several times before. "Just waiting for the chief."

She nodded. "You can just go on in. It sounded important." But before he could stand, she said, "How was that last callout? I never know what to think when it's announced as a 'person trapped.'"

Julio was only willing to say, "We got him out and off to the hospital."

She knew what that meant—the implication of what he hadn't said. "I'll tell the guys we are having pizza delivered tonight."

"Good idea."

She always sprung extra for the good stuff from Backdraft rather than franchise pizza that tasted the same no matter what city you are in.

Julio knocked on the desk and headed for Greyson's office. He slowed at the door.

The chief waved him in with his free hand. "Thank you, sir." Then he hung up the phone. "Have a seat."

"Thanks, Chief." Julio slumped into the seat, knowing what Greyson would ask first before they even got to what this was about. "We got the guy out, but Max and Prichard had to dismantle the entire machine. He probably won't be able to keep his arm, but he's alive and he will eventually be able to go home to his children."

Greyson nodded. "Sounds like you guys did a good job."

On top of that, things were good right now with Samantha. Two nights ago, he had kissed her good night and gone home to sleep like the dead until his shift. She was at home resting, probably working on her computer from her house. He'd worked a twenty-four-hour shift that ended earlier this morning—a couple of hours ago actually.

Not many of the guys complained about overtime, especially when they hadn't had many callouts for the duration of the shift. It just so happened that the last one overlapped the end of their time clocked in. Julio considered this morning's work on shift with the other firefighters as a win, even if it had gone longer than they were supposed to be working.

There was a hopefulness inside him centered on the new day. Something in him had settled, questions had been answered.

The thing that had always been between him and Samantha was at least somewhat resolved. Or, he simply woke up yesterday, or this morning, more observant of the new mercies available to him than he had been for a long time. The verse of the day that popped up on his Bible app this morning came from Lamentations chapter 3.

Great is thy faithfulness.

So why did he feel like Greyson was about to drop a bomb and ruin all of it? At least Julio had the training necessary to diffuse the device. But not if it was about to explode before he could do damage control.

"Yesterday afternoon, Detective Jesse received an email from the arsonist," Greyson began. "She wasn't logged in to her work computer at the time, so the email bounced to the on-call cop in the Intelligence Division on duty, which happened to be her boss, Sergeant Deerdan. They managed to move the email before she could read it."

"So she doesn't know?"

"It's my understanding she's being pulled into a meeting this morning, and that's when they're going to show it to her."

At least that was something. He couldn't imagine getting sent something and not being the first to know. Then again, just because she was a police detective with active cases didn't mean Samantha wasn't allowed to take time off and disconnect from her job in order to heal from the injuries she sustained getting attacked. There had to be some kind of coverage for the unexpected while an officer wasn't available to deal with them.

"When do you meet with the taskforce next?" Greyson asked.

"Lunchtime today." Julio wasn't entirely sure when he was supposed to sleep, but thankfully had at least four hours last night. It would do for now.

"Presume that might get shifted to include the FBI and more cops."

"So this is serious," Julio said. "What did the email say?" He didn't want to jump to conclusions before he even knew how bad the situation was, but if the arsonist had written her a note, there was a reason why.

Greyson handed over a piece of paper.

Julio scanned the text, first frowning and then unable to keep his eyes from widening. "You may *believe* you know who I am? What does that mean?" He didn't expect Greyson to answer, just kept reading. "*We will meet again.* Oh, I don't like the sound of that at all."

"No one does." Greyson sighed. "I'm pretty sure the police department and the arson taskforce are all in on making sure Samantha doesn't wind up the target. Given how he's wording things and rambling, we aren't dealing with a stable person." He lifted his hand, palm out. "Not that I'm an expert about mental conditions, but in my opinion, this is the writing of someone who's unstable."

"Agreed." Julio wanted to crumple the paper in his hands and throw it, but what would that serve? This guy had fixated on Samantha. Or at least recognized her as the one he wanted to approach.

Why couldn't he have chosen Julio?

That would absolutely have been his preference, not just to save the woman he cared about from being in the spotlight. *Okay, fine.* That might be pretty much the only reason. But who would blame him? No guy wanted to feel powerless while a possibly psychotic person was focused on the one they cared about more than anyone else.

Any guy worth his salt would gladly stand between her and the threat.

"My guess?" Greyson said. "The FBI's behavioral analysis-profiler person, whatever you call it, will be at the meeting. They'll add to the other information on our arsonist, which might give them a stronger impression of who this guy is. Maybe enough to identify him."

Julio figured that might be wishful thinking. Still, in this he would much rather be wrong. "I hope so." He put the paper facedown on the desk and ran his hands down his face. "We need to figure out who this guy is before anyone else gets hurt."

"I'd suggest you focus on keeping Samantha safe, but that leaves Tennet heading up the search for the arsonist."

Julio nodded. Evidently, Greyson wasn't going to say it out loud, but neither of them currently had much confidence in the captain over the arson investigation department.

He didn't want Samantha to wind up like Mitchell, beat up and left for dead. She had already been attacked. What he needed to do was prevent anything worse from happening to her. He needed to keep her safe, and he wasn't going to trust that duty to anyone else.

He'd do the job God had given him from the beginning.

Greyson eyed him. "Have you thought about applying to work in the arson department?"

Julio didn't want to work under Tennet when they were the same rank. "Maybe someday, but not right now."

"I don't know how much more time Tennet has left in him. He jumped the gun with that press conference, labeling the arsonist a copycat."

Julio nodded. "I figured we would be talking about that whole mess during today's briefing."

Even if he would much rather be on the street trying to figure out who this guy was. But what leads did they have? If Mitchell woke up, they could at least get an ID on the guy who had attacked him. Then there was the detail following the man who had attacked Samantha, then been arraigned and released pending his trial.

As far as he could see, they had a whole lot of nothing.

When were they going to get a break in this case?

"Stick with it for now," Greyson said. "I can't guarantee what's gonna happen next. But focus on doing your job to the best of your ability—the way I know you will anyway. I get that everything in you wants to be all about protecting Samantha, but finding this arsonist and putting him away has the same effect. And will speak volumes for your career."

Julio nodded. "Thanks, Chief."

He headed out of Greyson's office, past his assistant, to the stairs. In his office, he grabbed his cell phone and called Samantha to see if she knew yet about the email the arsonist had sent to her. He listened to it ring, pacing the tiny office between the wall and the cot.

She never answered.

A few seconds later he got a text from her,

I'll talk to you at the briefing.

Julio tossed the phone on the bed. The captain who was supposed to be on shift now would be headed in soon enough, wanting to use this room. Meanwhile, Julio had three hours to burn until the meeting. He needed something to do. Like walk around one of the fire scenes and see what he could gather.

Decision made, he set the radio he wore on the desk and gathered his things. Shoving everything into his backpack so he could head out in his personal car. Praying the whole time that God would give him the mercy of answers, or some kind of lead. A way to figure out who this guy was.

Before someone else lost their life.

TWENTY

Samantha didn't look at Julio, even though he'd sat himself to her left, in her line of sight. Romeo was beside her, which only meant she could see that he was texting Bristol and wasn't aware of the turmoil going on in Samantha. Julio, however, constantly glanced at her. As if anyone in the room wouldn't realize that he needed to know how she was reacting to this.

At the head of the table to the right, FBI Special Agent Addie Franklin stood wearing a pantsuit and white shirt. She had her hair pulled back, and her makeup was understated. The telltale tiredness of having little kids at home was evident on her face.

"...and that's why we believe he is connected to some kind of religious organization." Addie was about to continue when she was cut off.

"Like some kind of cult?" The question came from the mayor's chief of staff.

"We don't know what church or group it is, or if he even belongs to any kind of organized religion."

The chief of staff said, "How do you know for sure it's a man?"

Romeo looked up from his phone. "We arrested him two days ago."

"And yet he's already back on the streets." The chief of staff shot Romeo a look.

"That's how the justice system works," Romeo said. "We don't keep people detained just because we don't like them. You of all people should know how much it costs the city to keep the jail running."

Samantha shifted in her seat. They didn't need to get into a debate about funding for municipal services. Even if it would be a good distraction.

She had fought constantly through this entire briefing to keep her thoughts from becoming overwhelming. Just the idea that the arsonist was now fixated on her, or at least even minutely focused, was pretty much terrifying as a concept. Any more than that would threaten her sanity.

But having Julio here, clearly concerned about how she was handling the whole thing, helped her keep a handle on herself. If only so that no one knew the extent to which she was spiraling.

Lord, maybe I need Your help to hold it together.

It wasn't entirely comfortable yet for her to pray, but she was willing to test the theory that the God she knew was up there might be inclined to act on her behalf. She and Bristol had a long conversation about the whole thing yesterday.

Her sister attended a Bible study for the deaf, and always went to Sunday services. She'd been eager to share what she knew about what Samantha was supposed to do next—a mishmash of things. Right now, it was all mostly confusing—but in a way also seemed intriguing.

The idea that she could draw strength from something other than herself sounded good when Samantha had no reserves left. When things were out of control.

Still, it felt like trying to do your taxes in the middle of a shootout. There was entirely too much going on, your life was in danger, and at the same time you were supposed to do math? Okay, so the concept of Christianity wasn't exactly like an equation that needed solving in the middle of a life-and-death situation, but it also kind of was. Not just that, but she didn't have time for self-reflection right now.

"Speaking of the man that was arrested. Bill Morrison is on record as having applied to the Benson Fire Department twelve years ago."

Everyone looked at Addie.

The FBI agent in charge continued, "It's one of the few things we could find out about him. He seems to do construction and get paid under the table, which he uses to pay his rent with cash. There is little electronic record of him."

Captain Tennet said, "But you found the application?"

Addie nodded. "He was interviewed once as part of the application process and dismissed following that. I have the names of the officers who conducted the interview if you'd like to follow up with them."

"I'll do that," Tennet said. "It could prove fruitful."

Samantha spoke up. "Do we have any other suspects if it shakes out that the man who attacked me on the street isn't our arsonist?"

Addie looked at her. "All I can do is put together a

comprehensive profile of the type of person you're going to find. It will confirm what we suspect after the arrest has been made. What it doesn't do is single out a likely suspect."

Samantha's phone buzzed.

She jerked so hard the phone hit her coffee cup and some of the liquid sloshed out onto the table. She winced. So much for keeping her attention to herself. But if this was an email from the arsonist?

She braced and looked at the screen.

"What is it?" Julio asked.

Thankfully, not another manifesto in her email. Samantha was actually glad she hadn't been the one to open the email. Deerdan hadn't beat around the bush. She'd explained it in a way that allowed Samantha to absorb the blow with no one else around. As far as Deerdan was concerned, a threat directed at one officer in the department meant it was directed at every single officer who served.

She might be the target, but that kind of all-for-one thinking did help.

"It's the girlfriend of Mitchell Sylvana," Samantha replied. "She said he's awake enough we can go talk to him. Apparently, he has something to tell us."

Julio pushed back his chair. "Let's go."

As if she wasn't going to take Romeo with her and conduct a police interview. No, Julio had decided that the two of them were going to team up. She nearly smiled.

Samantha wished she had a good reason to tell him it was a terrible idea. But the problem was, given the way he'd been with her the last few days, she didn't have any reasons left to push him away.

She had a whole lot of reasons to hold on tight.

Captain Tennet cleared his throat.

Before he could start, Special Agent Franklin said, "This morning I spoke with the commissioners over both the fire department and the police department. I will be taking command of this taskforce until such time as the arsonist is arrested."

Everyone in the room shifted and glanced at her. Tennet stiffened in his seat, a pinched look on his face. Samantha didn't know what was going on, but it did seem like this taskforce needed more focus. Better leadership. If that came from an FBI expert in profiling, she was all for it.

Julio seemed to think it was a good idea as well, given the expression on his face. Something else they were on the same page about. Which only got her thinking about him kissing her goodbye two nights ago. How had his shift been that he'd worked between then and now? He didn't look tired, but then again he never seemed to feel the effects of tough work.

Addie said, "All reports will be sent directly to me. Tasks will be assigned by me, and no one is to give out any information without my express permission." She looked around the room. "Is that understood by everyone?"

Samantha said, "Understood."

Several of the others agreed, but Captain Tennet just sat stoically in his seat.

Addie said, "Captain Tennet, you and I will go over all of the fire scenes."

Julio lifted a finger. "I have some photos from this morning I'll send over."

"Very good," Addie said. "Captain Espinoza-Vasquez and Detective Jesse, go speak with Mitchell Sylvana. Find out what he has to say. Detective Alvarez, where are you at?"

"Two more interviews of warehouse staff to go. But they aren't giving me very much. Apparently, the parent company told them not to reveal anything about the class action suit. At least not until we can prove it's relevant."

"Stick with it. Report to me when you're done." She gave out a couple of other assignments to personnel in the room and then said, "You are all dismissed."

Samantha met up with Julio in the hallway, and they walked together to the elevator. Inside, he said, "Do I need to ask how you're doing with all this?"

"Let's just work the case and keep moving forward."

"As long as we keep our eyes open as well."

She glanced over at him.

"You know I have your back, right?"

"I know." She squeezed his arm.

Julio drove to the hospital, while Samantha scrolled through emails and chatted with Bristol over texts. But distracting herself would only serve a purpose for so long. Eventually, she had to actually pay attention to what was going on around her, mostly so she didn't get blindsided again like she had with that man. Was he out there, watching her?

Waiting to attack her again?

Her throat closed reflexively, and she had to swallow against the sensation. All she could think was that eventually she would be healed. The guy would be in cuffs and the case closed. The only thing left of it would be this thing between her and Julio that seemed to have flared back to life.

As they walked through the hospital lobby to the

elevator, she felt his fingers brush hers, but he didn't take her hand.

On the floor where Mitchell's room was, Julio motioned ahead of them. "That's her."

The woman had dark hair and a few inches of stomach visible below her cropped T-shirt. Her slightly rounded abdomen made Samantha wonder if she was pregnant. Had she and Mitchell made a baby together?

She'd known enough about religion at the time to know what she and Julio had done was wrong. Or at least, not in the right order—not blessed by God. But all that had done was pile shame and guilt on top of the grief she'd already been forced to carry. So that her strength buckled under the load.

Instead of finding comfort in what she knew to be true, she'd fallen apart in a mess of condemnation.

Something else she was going to have to figure out as she got to know God like a close friend, or a loving Father. Something she'd never quite grasped before. He always had seemed more like a distant figure in the sky, ready to smite her for the slightest infraction.

Julio said, "This is Terri." He gestured at Sam. "This is Detective Jesse. She's on the arson taskforce with me."

She stuck her hand out. "You can call me Samantha."

The other woman grasped her hand for a second, then let go. "He really wanted to talk to you, so thanks for coming."

Julio said, "Of course."

He went in first, and Samantha let Terri go ahead of her, closing the door behind her just in case anyone was loitering in the hallway. She'd worked a case once where a reporter snuck around behind her everywhere and tried to listen in on all kinds of conversations to get an exclusive.

Mitchell Sylvana looked a whole lot better than the last time she'd seen him. Not just because she'd thought at first glance that he was dead, and right now with his eyes open and more color in his cheeks than before, he was most definitely alive.

The other woman went to the side of the bed and placed her fingers in Mitchell's, standing beside him.

Mitchell looked at Samantha. "Thanks for coming, both of you."

She nodded.

Julio said, "We're hoping you can provide us with information about the man who attacked you."

Samantha tugged out her phone, where she had a photo of the man who had attacked her on the street. But she didn't show it to him yet. "Do you believe you're still in danger from him?"

"That's what we wanted to talk to you about," Mitchell said. "While he beat me, he told me everything."

TWENTY-ONE

Julio studied the man lying in the hospital bed. And the body language between him and Terri— most likely his girlfriend. That made him wonder if anyone thought the same about him and Samantha. Whether someone could tell from looking at them how they felt about each other.

He wasn't sure anyone else could tell how much strain she was under. Samantha kept a tight lid on her true feelings, refusing to let anyone know how she really felt. But even without the bruising on her neck, he would have been confident she needed someone with her. Just for support.

Whether she really was the target of this arsonist, or someone else looking to get payback—or simply an unfortunate set of circumstances and mistaken intentions— didn't matter.

He was here for her.

Samantha showed Mitchell the screen of her phone. "First of all, could you tell me, is this the man who attacked you?"

Probably a photo of the guy that also attacked her. Bill Morrison. The one Julio had put cuffs on, something far more satisfying than he'd expected. Then again, it wasn't more satisfying than putting out a fire or being there to save someone's life. The fact it involved Samantha and keeping her safe probably made a difference.

Mitchell shook his head. "No, that's not him. I don't know that guy."

"You're certain?" She asked. "He wasn't wearing a mask, or some other kind of face covering?"

"I saw his face. I know exactly what he looks like, and that's not him." He stiffened, shifting on the bed. Whether the pain was a result of his injuries or remembering what happened to him didn't much matter. Either way, he'd have to deal with it until it healed and the memories faded.

Samantha slid her phone back into her pocket. "He said he told you everything?"

"Most of it was crazy ranting." Mitchell winced. "It's hard to piece it all together, but I'll tell you what I can."

"It doesn't matter if it's disjointed," Julio said. "We just need to know as much as you can recall."

Samantha nodded. "Just start with what stuck out to you the most and fill in the gaps as you go."

"The guy's crazy ranting is what *stuck out to me* the most." Mitchell made a face. "A whole lot of stuff that sounded like it came from the Bible." His gaze took on a faraway expression, his dark eyes shadowed. "He told me I had to call him Richard. Can you believe that? Like he really believes he is my old man. He kept calling me *Son*, but then he was also saying how we were brothers, but he was superior."

"To your knowledge, are you related to him?" Samantha asked.

Mitchell shook his head. "I'd never seen the guy before. I don't think I have any uncles or siblings. Not on my dad's side."

Julio figured that the taskforce should dig into any possibilities Mitchell wasn't aware of. Just in case their arsonist really was related to Sylvana.

Mitchell continued, "He just sounded crazy. That's all I can think of. How crazy it was. He said he was Richard, then he said he was the 'son of promise.' He was calling me Ishmael, like that was some kind of demerit. Or insult."

Samantha glanced over. "Why does that sound familiar?"

"From Genesis. Ishmael was the son of the servant, from when Abraham was trying to bring God's promise to fruition in his own strength. Using his own plan to achieve the same end. The son of promise was the true heir."

Julio didn't recall much more specifics than that. There were some names he couldn't remember, as it had been a long time since he read the Bible. More than two years in fact. He really needed to start getting back into that again, considering how far he'd come the last few days. Managing to let go of a lot of his anger.

If God really had brought him and Samantha back together for a reason, then he needed to get back into the Bible.

He and Samantha needed to do things differently this time, living out their faith. Not just saying they believed and then going about their life in a way that made them effectively hypocrites. At the least they hadn't acted in accordance with what they said they believed last time.

There were a lot of things he had to get straight in his head or figure out how to deal with. But he knew two things: God was real, and Samantha was the only woman he had ever loved.

He figured the rest of it would work itself out in time.

Mitchell said, "There's something you guys need to know." He glanced at Terri. "Something he found out when he was looking around my house. After he tied me up, he knocked me out, and when I came around, he was looking at papers. He found an invoice from a doctor in the house."

Terri paled. She reached out and held Mitchell's hand.

"Terri is having a baby. My baby. He started asking about the baby, and then ranting about how it wasn't supposed to go down like that. How he was the one who was supposed to have the heir."

"It seems like he might be mixed up about a whole lot of things." Julio couldn't even begin to decipher what Mitchell was saying this man believed. Added to the manifesto that had been emailed to Samantha, with its religious connotations, their arsonist came off like a true believer.

In something very scary.

Samantha nodded. "Did he mention anything about what his plans are next?"

Now that they were fairly sure her attacker wasn't the same man who had hurt Mitchell, that meant they were looking for someone else. The police detail watching that man might as well go home. Although, if he contacted the arsonist, they would need to know. Especially if he met the person face-to-face.

Could Bill Morrison have been paid to attack Samantha like that?

"I can't help but think that he might try and hurt Terri," Mitchell said. "He was so angry, ranting about her. He even asked me where she lived and where she worked. But I didn't tell him. That's when he went too far and left me for dead."

Terri sucked in a breath. Fighting tears, which were completely understandable in the circumstances.

Samantha said, "What else can you remember of what he said?"

"He just kept talking about how he was going to become the father. As if I was supposed to know what that meant. But then he was telling me to call him Richard, or Dad, like he believes he's my father. He started ranting about becoming even more. Like...I can't remember what word he used."

So far, the arsonist had been targeting people who were connected to Richard Sylvana's original case. Then he had come after the man's son.

Julio was going to worry about himself and do what he could to protect the innocent from those who hurt them. Generally that was centered around fires, but he was leaning into this taskforce thing, and helping Samantha with her police department duties. People like Terri and her baby would be safe because they were working this case.

Mitchell looked at Terri. "When I get released from the hospital, I want to be in protective custody. I know no one is going to want to keep Richard Sylvana's son safe, but with the baby, maybe someone will be inclined to help us. I don't want to have to face that guy again, and if he comes after us both...?" He turned to Samantha.

She nodded. "I'll contact my sergeant and get someone assigned to you. Who your father is doesn't have any bearing on who you are, and it certainly doesn't make you less worthy of our help."

"Thank you." Mitchell's voice sounded choked.

"Do you think you could look through some images and see if you can point out the man who attacked you?"

Mitchell gave a little shrug. "Maybe, I mean...it's worth a try at least."

"Thank you," Samantha said. "An officer will come over with a computer so you can look at mugshots. We could really use your help trying to identify this man."

Terri shifted in her seat, looking a little more relieved than she had minutes ago.

"I'm going to make that call now, so we don't leave you here unprotected." Samantha moved to the door and stepped out into the hallway.

Julio knew that hospitals had decent security, and Mitchell could be transferred to a floor that was only accessible through a locked door. They could involve hospital security in keeping Mitchell and Terri safe.

Julio turned to the mother-to-be. "Are you okay to stay here?" They could drive her to her home so she could get some of her things if necessary. But he also wanted to get out there and keep trying to figure out who the arsonist was.

Terri gestured at a backpack in the corner. "I have some things with me. Just in case."

"Okay." To Mitchell he said, "Did the man who attacked you say anything about the fires that he set? Or any that he might be planning to set in the future?"

The other man frowned, thinking it through. "It was just a lot of ranting. I was in and out, and he kept hitting me."

"Because he was angry at you?"

"I think he's mad that I'm Richard's son and he isn't. But then, he thinks he is Richard and he's planning on becoming something else." Mitchell's expression shifted, total confusion on his face. "Maybe he mentioned some of the fires, but I was so out of it that I don't really remember."

"Will you tell the police if you remember anything else?"

Mitchell nodded. "I can do that. I really hope you guys find him."

"Me, too."

Samantha stepped back in the room. "Security is coming up. They'll stay in the hall until two police officers get here. Your room is going to be constantly under guard until this man is caught."

Terri said, "Thank you both."

They all shook hands, and Julio and Samantha stepped into the hall. He checked his phone, since he had silenced it before they stepped inside the room. The sight of all the notifications made him stop walking in the middle of the hallway.

Samantha leaned in, close to his side. Her hand on his arm. "What is it?"

"There's another fire in progress. A summer sports event at a school, so there are multiple kids trapped inside a gym."

She squeezed his arm. "Let's go."

"There isn't anything we can do without gear. And you're not a firefighter." He wasn't going to let her put her life in danger more than it already was. She'd already been a target of this guy once—or so he figured. Whatever the reason Bill Morrison attacked her.

"Maybe not, but we can help outside, and we might see him hanging around."

He figured he could keep her from doing a lot of helping. Considering she was still recovering from being attacked, she needed to take it easy. "Fine. Let's go. But you're going to stay back."

He'd rather she was as far from this guy as possible, but that wouldn't help them take him down.

Just as soon as they figured out who he was.

TWENTY-TWO

"I'm not going to go in there and leave you alone out here, unprotected."

Samantha stared up at Julio, and the concern in his features. "There are a lot of people here, and they could probably use your help."

She wasn't going to remind him that she had a gun and was able to take care of herself. Considering how quickly she had been subdued by that guy, and the fact he could have easily killed her if it wasn't for Julio showing up, she wasn't going to argue the point.

But he had a job to do.

The parking lot in front of the school was an ocean of people and vehicles, flashing red and blue lights. They had called in on the way over, and one of the fire chiefs told Julio that all thirty-five of the kids were trapped inside, smoke pouring out of the windows, and the firefighters were having trouble gaining access to the building.

Who knew what the situation was inside.

As for what they did know, this was most likely the

work of their arsonist, considering the way the building had been secured. Trapping all the victims inside. The chief had told them that the doors looked like liquid cement had been squeezed into the locks to set like rock. The doorframes were sealed tight with something, so they were having to break through exterior walls.

Samantha couldn't see any flames in the building, from the fire no doubt blazing inside. But then again, she was a cop and not a firefighter, so it could be out of sight. Julio hadn't said anything about the visible smoke or the fact there was no fire.

"Go be a captain." She squeezed his arms. "That's what they need you to do right now."

Julio leaned down and kissed her quickly, then raced toward the building. He disappeared between two vehicles. Past a fire truck and what seemed like an ocean of people.

Samantha looked around, aware of being alone even with all these people. No wonder he hadn't wanted to leave her. The truth was, she would rather go with him. But in this situation, she would only be in the way.

Right now, she wanted to see if she could recognize any of the spectators and bystanders.

She skirted the edge of the crowd and spotted a police officer she knew working crowd control. He lifted his chin, and she did the same in return. Before she could ask him how things were going, her cell phone rang.

Sergeant Deerdan's name flashed on the screen.

Samantha slid her thumb across and put it to her ear. "Jesse."

"I did some more digging, figured you would want an update. Are you at the school?"

"Yes. Is Alvarez finished with his interviews? I

might need some backup." Samantha figured Romeo might want to be here as well, and she could use someone with her as she looked around. No sense going face-to-face with this guy on her own when she didn't have to because she had the backing of somebody she trusted.

Meanwhile, Julio was free to do his fire captain duties without having to worry about her.

The sergeant said, "I'll text him and tell him to get over there. I think he's wrapping up."

"Thanks."

"As for my update, I looked into the man who attacked you, Bill Morrison." She said that as if she never would have believed that Samantha had started the fight. "He actually changed his name a few years ago, so we didn't have completely accurate information on him."

Samantha gripped the phone and tried to keep at least part of her attention on the people around her so she didn't get blindsided again. "Who is he?"

"Four years ago, he was Walter Barnes. You interviewed him, but you spent more time with his wife."

"Marianne Barnes."

And yet, Bill Morrison had attempted to join the FD twelve years ago? Now he was back to using that name again.

"That's right," Deerdan said. "She was a domestic violence victim. Walter was the perpetrator, and I believe you counseled her to leave since she wasn't prepared to press charges."

"I remember straight up telling her if she stayed, he would end up killing her."

"Seems like she left." Deerdan paused. "Or completely dropped off the radar, at least."

"How do we know he didn't kill her and hide the body?"

"We won't until the two detectives I assigned to investigate confirm for sure that she is safe, or manage to find enough evidence for an arrest warrant."

Samantha winced. "I'm going to pray she got herself together and managed to escape rather than that he might have killed her."

"Considering he seems angry at you, I'm going to air on the side of believing she left and he doesn't know where she is. Or never bothered to find her."

"So why did he attack me?"

"We would have to get him to confess that someone paid him to sucker you into that fight."

Samantha made a face. "Right. I don't see him harboring all this anger at me for years and then suddenly making his move." There were other far more effective ways to do that.

More likely, the arsonist found someone with a grudge against her and used that as leverage for his own ends.

To throw them off his trail.

She lifted a hand to her throat reflexively and touched the bruising she still had there. She swallowed and it was still scratchy. Eventually, the injuries would heal, and she would barely remember the look on his face when he'd been trying to choke her to death.

Deerdan said, "I agree it's more likely he was paid or convinced to come after you. Possibly by the arsonist. Maybe he's been following you for a while, or whoever this guy is found someone in your past willing to come after you."

Samantha recalled how Romeo had been under the

impression someone was following them the other day. "Hopefully, he hasn't convinced more than one person to do that." Otherwise, she would be constantly looking over her shoulder. Or hiding in her house.

"The officers with Mitchell and Terri report everything is quiet over there, so at least that is taken care of. I'll get Romeo over to your location so you aren't without backup."

"Thanks, Sarge."

"Keep me updated." Deerdan hung up.

Samantha studied the crowd, her mind spinning about Marianne Barnes and her fate. She prayed the woman had found safety rather than a violent end to her life. Walter probably changed his name so he could skate out from under responsibility, or he'd been finding it difficult to get a job. Or it was all about making it harder for the police or anyone else to figure out who he was? Seemed like he went back and forth, and he might even have more aliases—possibly even one with an outstanding warrant.

She would have just moved to another city if it were her, but people made all kinds of choices when they thought they had no other option.

Like breaking up with Julio because she hadn't believed that they could possibly have a future with a loss like that between them. All the guilt and shame.

She hadn't seen another way out.

Samantha wandered through the crowd, making eye contact with as many people as she could. One of the firefighters in uniform, wearing a white shirt but not a high rank, held a video camera. Taking footage of everyone in the crowd so they could watch it later and confirm whether the arsonist was here or not.

It might only be evidence admitted in court after they caught the guy, but as far as she was concerned, every little piece was worth gathering. The more nails in his coffin the better.

She wandered far enough she got to the other end of the high school building. As she got there, she spotted a couple of bystanders running down the side of the building and jogged after them.

She got close enough to see a man with a tire iron attempting to open a side door. He grasped the metal and tried to pry the door away from the lock. Two women stood beside him. All of them looked scared and desperate.

She told them, "If you need to get inside, we can speak with the fire department. They have tools for this." Never mind that they shouldn't be trying to get into a burning building.

The man ignored her, his face reddened as he strained to open the door.

Samantha looked at the women. The one with curled blond hair and a round figure said, "Our kids are in there. Their phones are on this side of the building." She lifted her own cell phone and showed Samantha where a dot-like GPS location blinked on the screen. "We have to get them out."

"This door won't budge." The man looked out the tire iron, and it clattered to the concrete by his feet. "It must be sealed shut somehow."

Samantha looked at the handle, below which something gray covered the lock. She touched it with her finger. "The firefighters are aware. It's some kind of dried cement." She needed to get these people back to where the other spectators were. "They're getting everybody out to the front door. It's best that we let them do their jobs."

The brunette gasped. "Emily is calling me!" She put her phone to her ear. "Honey, are you inside the building? Can you get to a door?"

Samantha pulled out her phone and texted Julio to tell him that these people were trying to get inside

The brunette told her daughter, "We're trying to get in, but the doors are all locked. Can you break a window?" She lowered the phone a few seconds later. "She said the windows upstairs are all locked as well. The teacher has them in lockdown, huddled in closets. But it's smoky, and they don't want to be there."

"If you can tell the firefighters where they are, it will help them reach the kids faster." Samantha needed these people to stand down trying to get inside and work with the fire department, not in spite of them. "Let the first responders do their jobs."

The man swept up the tire iron with a huff. "I'm going to see if I can find a window myself. No one is waiting for the firefighters to get off their butts and get a door open." He wandered away toward the back of the building.

Samantha looked back at the two women. "Can you go tell the firefighters where the kids are?"

The blonde looked where the man had gone, then raced off after him.

The brunette on the phone seemed locked in indecision. She shifted the phone back in front of her mouth. "I know, honey. Someone is coming to get you out soon."

Samantha's phone buzzed, and she saw the message from Julio. Her eyes widened.

"What is it?" the brunette asked. "What just happened?"

"There isn't any fire in the building, just smoke."

"What does that mean? What's happening?"

"I don't know," Samantha said, "but I'm going to try and find out." She headed for the front of the building, figuring this was the best way of getting at least one of these parents to the right area.

The other woman came with her, talking to her daughter on the phone. The first firefighter Samantha saw, she directed to the woman. "This lady is speaking with one of the students inside."

"Thanks." He nodded. "Ma'am, this way!"

Samantha left them and continued walking, headed for the center of a cluster of firefighters who looked like the ones in charge. Scanning the area for Julio, she spotted him speaking with another man—a chief—and Captain Tennet, as well as a few others.

Instinct felt like cold fingers on her spine. Samantha glanced around, aware she felt as if she were being watched.

Walter Barnes wasn't in police custody anymore.

Was he here, watching her?

Or was it the arsonist?

She didn't understand why she was the target. How could she be a threat to the arsonist's plans? The only thing that had changed in her life recently was the fact Julio was back in it. Could that be the change which triggered the attention?

Perhaps this was about distracting Julio so that he didn't see the truth.

Samantha was going to figure it out, whatever the answer was.

Hopefully before someone else got hurt.

TWENTY-THREE

Julio pushed the outer layers of the onion off the cutting board and got to work chopping the middle. It would take some prep work, but he needed to get this Mexican chicken soup in the Instant Pot in time. If he did, the firefighters working overtime could come into the firehouse and find a flavorful meal waiting for them. After all those hours doing cleanup, and coordinating with other agencies, they would be more than ready for a meal by the time they returned.

He glanced over at Samantha, who sat on one side of the long dining table in the firehouse kitchen. Poring over files Captain Tennet had dropped off earlier that day. The original arson case against Richard Sylvana.

But all Julio could think about was the fire at the school just now—or more accurately, the lack of fire. As far as he could tell, the incident had been caused by a few smoke bombs strategically placed by the HVAC intakes so that the ashy-colored smoke filtered through the whole building.

Anyone would have believed it was on fire, especially with the heating turned up so high.

Warm air had been pumping through the air vents for hours before the first alarm sounded. Kids trapped inside, unable to get out through doors that had been secured shut. It would take days to figure out precisely what had happened. By then, he hoped they'd have found the identity of the arsonist and arrested him. But all he could do right now was pray, make soup, and let Samantha see what she could find in those files.

Julio stirred onion and peppers in the skillet, browning them so he could put them in the soup.

Samantha made a noise low in her throat, and he glanced over. "Find something?"

"Unfortunately, nothing about locking doors so people can't get out. That seems to be something this arsonist likes to do but not the original. Maybe he has different resources, or he likes feeling like he outsmarted us. It's probably so the victims suffer maximum panic when they realize they can get out." She shuddered. "But get this. With the first two fires set by Richard Sylvana, one was a residence, and a woman died like recently in the other. Later, the original arsonist set fire to a warehouse, with no one inside...unlike our fire where the lawyer perished."

"So he's following the same pattern? That was our theory. Until the manifesto."

Samantha tipped her head to the side. "Not entirely the same pattern, but it's close enough Tennet wanted to announce he'd figured out it was a copycat. But the original arsonist did set a fire at a prom, trapping a bunch of kids in the gym of their school."

"Not exactly like what happened today," Julio said.

"But he's re-creating it close enough that we might be able to figure out where he will hit next."

"Could just be that school isn't in this week." She glanced over. "He doesn't want to wait for prom season."

Julio wondered if she was remembering their prom.

She continued, "According to this, with one of his next fires he tried to burn down a firehouse."

Julio looked around. Okay, so not thinking about their prom.

There was no one else here but them, making the firehouse quiet in a way it rarely was. After hours, the civilian staff, who worked regular office shifts, headed out for the day. The firefighters who worked around the clock were all on a callout, including the EMTs who bunked in the building next door.

He flipped off the burner, which sputtered for a second and then went out. Then dumped the onion and peppers in the Instant Pot and pulled the package of chicken out, slicing it while he thought about the case. A firehouse?

If the arsonist was going to choose one, no doubt it would be Julio's.

Once the chicken was in the Instant Pot, he washed up. "I'll do a walkthrough when I'm done here, see if I can find any evidence something is going to happen."

Samantha flipped over a page.

Julio took a file from beside her, but when he stared at it, all he saw was a blur of text. His mind didn't want to let go of what the arsonist could possibly have achieved by trapping those kids in a building. It wasn't like there had actually been a fire. More like someone had wanted it to look like there was.

Maybe a kid causing trouble? Not their arsonist at all.

Someone trying to get back at them, the way Walter Barnes had with Samantha. She'd told him all about that on their drive from the scene back to the firehouse. Her whole case with the guy and his wife, now missing. The second he had suggested they make dinner for the rest the crew, she jumped at the chance to leave and get to safety.

Regroup.

He couldn't help but think she had been nervous about being out in the open. As far as he was concerned, keeping her safe was his number one job right now. She didn't need to be worried.

Walter Barnes was on the street, though, and clearly had it in for Samantha. Julio wasn't sure he was entirely convinced by Mitchell and his story about him and Terri being in danger because of the baby.

Not that he thought the man was lying, but that it was far too easy to label the arsonist religious nut job. All that rambling? It spoke more of pathology.

Had Mitchell been lying? He could be working with the guy and later tried to back out or crossed him somehow so the person—some kind of partner—retaliated.

No one became something horrible in a vacuum. People just didn't live that disconnected from others these days. So if this guy was a true believer and an arsonist, then someone along the line had to have noticed there was something wrong with him.

Or that was simply wishful thinking.

If Julio's theory was true, there would be someone to blame for the arsonist's actions.

Maybe it was better to put all the responsibility on the man who committed the crimes—after they identified him, and he was brought to justice.

Samantha leaned over, her vanilla scent teasing his

senses. "Is there anything in that file about doors being secured shut and trapping people inside?"

Julio hadn't even started reading it. He glanced at her, giving himself a moment to simply absorb the fact she was close to him. He had her back in his life when she hadn't been for two years. They had a fresh start, a second chance to begin new and hopefully do things better this time. Like get it right and make this thing between them last the rest of their lives.

"Why are you looking at me like that?" she asked.

"Because I missed you." Julio leaned close and kissed her, expressing all the longing from the last two years in the way his lips moved over hers. Kind of like how she had, in the truck.

All her frustration and fear poured into a kiss.

Now, he was giving her the depth of how he felt. The way they connected in such a simple way, but with so much profound meaning. All the spark and chemistry whipped up at first like a frenzy, like the heat of the blaze. And then when it settled, they were left with the comfort of warmth. The kind of connection that would last the rest of their lives.

When he leaned back, she smiled slightly, her cheeks pink. "I missed you, as well."

"I'm glad we got that straight between us."

"Me, too, because we're supposed be working right now."

He flashed back to high school when they should have been studying for algebra. Instead, they had spent half an hour making out, using up all their time before he had to go home. So many times, they'd been distracted by each other enough they never got any work done. He wondered why he'd tried to study with her around at all.

"Why are you smiling?" she said.

He felt his lips widen in an all-out grin. "Just remembering algebra."

She rolled her eyes, a smile tugging at her lips. "This isn't high school."

"I'd say that's a shame, but I'm not sure those were the best years of our lives."

She laughed. "I've never agreed with that. I much prefer being responsible for my own life and not having to ask for money every time I need some."

"Right." He leaned back in his chair, turned slightly toward her. "There's something I should probably tell you."

She looked at him, a frown crinkling her brow. "What do you need to tell me?"

"Remember after..." He wasn't sure he was going to say that out loud. "We knew what we did could result in you being pregnant."

And it had.

He didn't want her to get swallowed up in grief again, so he said, "Remember how I brought you the listing for that house? I had just been promoted to lieutenant, and the pay raise was enough to swing the mortgage."

"We were both saving just in case. Figuring we would need a down payment for something at some point— together. And the money to pay for a wedding."

He nodded, not quite sure how to explain it without just being straightforward. "You seemed like you loved that house so much."

"Of course, I did. We did that tour, remember? It was gorgeous. Why are you talking about the house?"

"I bought it," Julio said. "I was going to tell you, but the explosion happened. I'd put down the earnest money a couple of days before. Then you were in hospital, and we didn't seem to be able to have a conversation without yelling at each other, so I just let it go."

"You didn't." She shook her head. "I pushed you away. I told you never to come back."

"Maybe I thought at some point you would. That we would be us again."

"So you went through with it?"

Julio winced. "I kind of waited too long and then couldn't back out of it. But I didn't really want to, so it isn't as if I actually tried. I wanted to give you what you wanted when you came back." As crazy as it was, maybe he'd been waiting for her this whole time.

"You live there?"

"Two years now." He nodded. "I've repainted every room, made some upgrades in my spare time. I put a deck on the back. Remember when we said that?"

It had taken some time to start fixing it up. All the grief over the baby and their breakup had soured him on the house at first. But after a while with nothing to do on his time off but sit around an empty house, he'd realized that he could channel his frustration and energy into making the house his. Even if it would never be...theirs.

"I can't believe you live in that house." Samantha blinked, an astonished look on her face.

"You should come and see it, maybe later. Or the first chance we get. I think you'll like what I did with it."

She sniffed back the tears rolling down her face.

Julio reached into the basket in the center of the table and snagged a napkin. "It's okay to be sad. We lost a lot, but we also found something that's worth holding onto."

"Now that we have it back, I don't want to lose it again." She dabbed her eyes with the napkin he handed to her. "But it's hard when I can't help thinking that every time I have something good, I never get to keep it. What's the point in enjoying it right now and trying to soak up the moments when I know there's no hope that it will be forever?"

She really thought that?

Samantha cleared her throat. "Aside from my sister, I've never had anything good that lasted. And even that was soured by my parents forcing me to always be the one to take care of her while she did whatever she wanted."

Bristol had been wild, and every time she got in trouble for pushing boundaries, Samantha had been blamed for the fallout. As if she was responsible for everything her sister did.

Julio touched her shoulder, trying to impart some comfort. "Maybe we should make a promise right here and now. You stick with me, and I stick with you. No matter what."

She studied him, biting the edge of her lip. "I want to, but it's still scary."

"Scarier than the idea of being without each other the rest of our lives?" The last two years were already bad enough. He gave her a second, then said, "What do you say?"

"I stick with you, and you stick with me?"

Julio nodded.

"Okay, you've got a deal."

"You're promising?"

"I promise," Samantha said.

He leaned in, intending to seal the pact with another kiss.

Before he got that far, thunder rumbled through the

building. A wall of flames rushed at them, flinging them out of their seats against the wall.

Samantha cried out.

Julio collided with something. He felt a wrenching pain in his shoulder, and everything washed in the wave of heat.

Fire.

TWENTY-FOUR

Richard stood on the roof of the medical center across the street, having gained access to the building with his credentials. They didn't know it was so he could watch the fire burn. He could smell the smoke from here, along with the tang of something new.

He was evolving.

To the east, under the gray afternoon sky, the firehouse had collapsed in on itself. The office wing was nothing but rubble. Unexpected, considering he'd placed one device on that side and another in the operations wing.

Trees on the sidewalk swayed in a gentle breeze. As if unaware that a fire blazed feet away, determined to spread. Left unchecked, it would eat its way through the city, consuming fuel with every foot it gained. Taking over. Taking control.

Would the whole city burn?

Richard shivered at just the thought of standing here, watching it all go up in flames.

He caught himself before he descended into the spiral of those rapturous thoughts.

He had to focus on this fire.

Today.

Not the next step.

One of his devices here must have malfunctioned, but that wasn't entirely surprising given explosives weren't his usual method of destruction.

He'd rather it would've been the other side of the building, where he had seen them enter. He'd placed the device close to the load-bearing wall between the kitchen and bunk rooms. But that side of the firehouse hadn't collapsed completely.

Richard watched flames lick up from the rubble on both sides.

If occupants weren't dead now, they would be soon enough.

The old, swept away in the fire of purification. Making way for the new.

He was aware the firefighters had made a number of reports about the condition of the building—at least compared to the brass and their fancy headquarters. Complaints of disrepair at the firehouse. Requests for materials to shore up the structure and bring it back to code. But budget cuts had scraped renovation plans. The department didn't want to fix what wasn't broken beyond their ability to repair.

At least now, they would be forced to completely redesign their response team's base of operations.

Only two lives lost in the tragedy.

He watched the flames pick up. Someone on the sidewalk below him pointed to the destruction, calling out to a friend. A phone was drawn out of a pocket. A frantic request made.

But it would take time for the response. After all, he'd perfectly timed it so the house would be mostly empty, as everyone else was occupied by the incident at the school. A fire extinguished before it could reach its full potential was far too disappointing.

He was better than that now.

Richard Sylvana was the past. He had become something more, the old washed away and made new. Creation. Rebirth.

Fire was the only way to accomplish what had to be.

And with the two of them working this case as part of the taskforce, it was only a matter of time before things came to a head.

And so he had dealt another blow—this one fatal.

TWENTY-FIVE

Samantha's throat still felt bruised from Walter's attack. Her mind flashed with an image of him above her, squeezing the life out of her. Determined to end her. She fought through the nightmare to consciousness. Aware something was wrong.

Very wrong.

Her nascent faith flared to life in a moment of fear, erupting into flame like a smolder coming to life. She needed that flame, the hope it brought with it rather than destruction. Fire meant warmth. It meant light in the darkness.

Lord, help us.

She didn't even know what she was praying for. Until she fought far enough through the haze to blink her eyes open. Everything rushed back in that instant.

Smoke filled the air. Darkness surrounded her, and she pulled in a breath she had to cough out.

Samantha recalled the explosion, that recent memory mixing with the time she'd been blown out of that house. The day she lost their baby.

Julio.

No words escaped her lips. She cried out for him in the recesses of her mind.

The firehouse.

They'd been at the table, and then everything washed in noise and heat. The past and the present collided in a wash of sensations. But unlike that day, Julio had been here with her. They'd been cooking. Looking at files. Trying to find an arsonist.

He'd found them.

Samantha took stock of herself first, as was that old adage: *Rescuer safety first.* She couldn't help anyone else if she was a victim.

Arms. Legs. Something lay on her left thigh. A heavy weight that wasn't drywall or the frame of the building.

She kept one hand on the weight pressing against her leg and dug for her phone. Had it been on the table, or was it...

There.

In her pocket, back right side where she usually kept it.

She dug the device out and squeezed the button on the side. The screen illuminated, nothing but shattered glass. At least, the backlight still worked. She pulled down the top menu and tapped on the flashlight, pretty sure she also cut her finger on the broken glass of the screen in the process.

Samantha let out a breath, now able to see around her. Around them.

She shined the phone around, lighting the small space between what looked like the table and a part of the wall that had collapsed. Which meant they were in a small space, against a load-bearing wall. In a pocket of air, such as it was.

She didn't think beyond that assessment.

No signal. No way to dial out, if she even could with the smashed screen.

"Julio." Her voice emerged, barely a whisper. Just the act of inhaling set her off into a fit of coughing.

He groaned, shifting very slightly in the small space. The weight on her eased and then increased a second later.

"Julio," she repeated, patting his shoulder. Then she shined the light on him and gasped, coughing some more.

Blood tracked down the side of his face. A lot of blood.

He was turned toward her, his shirt covered in dust.

"Sammy?"

"Yeah, I'm here."

He shoved up, leaning against her leg while he forced his upper body upright. It was at that point she saw the unnatural angle of his shoulder.

Samantha gasped. She coughed again.

Julio groaned. He slid his arm against his body with his other, holding it there while he looked around.

She used her phone to show him the space they were in.

"Side wall collapsed. Must've been a bomb." He inhaled through his nose. "Something ignited. Maybe the gas in the kitchen."

"There's a fire?" she croaked.

"We need to call out." He looked around, then at her. "Does your phone work?"

She handed it over, her head still full of everything.

Barely able to process what had happened and what they were going to do about it.

He looked at the screen. "It's busted. We might be able to get a callout, though." He tapped the screen, his other arm still tucked against his chest. "Maybe."

She stared at him. The man she had loved for as long as she could remember. The guy she had never stopped having feelings for, no matter how hard she tried.

Samantha shifted her legs, trying to move them now that he was off her.

The space around them groaned and shifted.

Julio's head jerked up. "Hold still."

"I don't know if I can. I need to move my legs." She gasped.

"I don't know if I got a callout." Julio set the phone aside, facedown so they could see the light.

He touched her cheek with his good hand. Just a brief glance of his warmth on her face, then his fingers sank into her hair. It took her a second, but she realized he was checking her for injury. Shoulders. Arms. "You're not bleeding anywhere as far as I can see. Which is a miracle."

Thank You, Lord.

"Amen to that."

She'd said it aloud?

"What about your legs?"

Samantha pulled her feet toward her, bringing her knees up. Nothing else around them shifted. Until she had settled, she didn't exhale. Then she was able to release the breath. "I feel okay. Just shaken."

Plus a whole lot of aches and pains that would probably feel like whiplash tomorrow. Bruises. But his shoulder was dislocated.

"Julio..." She motioned to it.

"I know. Don't worry about me. We need to get out of here or survive long enough for someone to reach us." He looked at the phone screen, the light turning to shine on the smashed photo beside him. Firefighters in aprons, holding a trophy. "Doesn't look like the call went through. But there's no way no one noticed what happened. Help will be here soon enough."

She figured that was true. But who wanted to be trapped, unable to get free and forced to do nothing until they were rescued?

At least when she'd been blown up before, she'd landed on grass outside. Unconscious until she woke up in the hospital and realized that everything she'd been thinking was her future in the minutes before the explosion had changed.

Her life had changed.

Samantha shivered.

Julio touched the back of his hand to her forehead. "You're in shock."

Was that why his hand felt far too warm?

He looked at her with that same concern. Like she couldn't handle things on her own and he needed to be with her. To stand in the gap. To take the blow for her. As if she wasn't strong enough for whatever life sent her way.

She could be strong.

"I'm fine," she stated.

"You seriously expect me to believe that?"

"I don't have a dislocated shoulder." That's probably why he wasn't currently trying to dig their way out. "Tell me what to do, and I'll get us out of here."

"We need to wait for rescue, Sammy."

"I don't like waiting."

"And yet, we've both been doing it for two years."

She whipped her head up to look at him. He wanted to talk about this now? Frustration and pain laced his features. She knew him well enough to know he had no filter right now. He needed to distract himself and taking a shot at her was the easiest. She was close to him. And he wanted a result—an end to the distance between them.

"You haven't dated anyone since." He waited at beat. "Have you?"

She wanted to lie and tell him she'd been swept away by something—anything—that proved as powerful as what was between them.

But she hadn't been.

"Have *you*?" she countered.

"I tried. I should admit that at least." Julio didn't quite meet her gaze. "I have dated. But nothing stuck, because they weren't you."

She didn't know what to say to that.

Julio leaned over so his face was close to hers. "You know how I feel. How I've always felt. Even when you were pushing me away, I knew it was just because you were in pain."

Tears burned in her eyes. The smoke. The wealth of emotion that had always been between them. She had never known what to do with the powerful feelings that just existed, tying them together.

Forever.

Samantha blinked, and twin tears rolled down her face. "Do we have to do this now?"

"I can't think of a better time when we have nothing else to do but sit here."

"And rehash everything?" Did she want that?

Yes, okay. She did.

More than anything.

But she'd never been able to keep the good things she had in her life. And if things with Julio ended again, what was she going to do? It had destroyed her before.

If they split up again, she would have nothing left.

"Do you want things to stay the way they are now? Or do you want something better?" Julio used his good hand to swipe a single tear from her cheek. "Because I don't want to live another day, if we even get the chance after this, without knowing you're in my life. That you know how I feel. That I wanted you always, no matter what. To raise a family with you and all that entails. The right way. Eventually, we'd get it right. Take our kids to church. Teach them to do better than make the mistakes we made."

Samantha sniffed. "It's been two years. Why does it still hurt like this?"

"I need you to let it go. To let the fear go and take a chance with me." He stared at her with so much warmth in his dark eyes. "Can you do that?"

Given everything Bristol had told her, she was pretty sure the only way to do that was with God's help. To let Him have the fear and the hurt. "I need to figure out how."

Julio nodded slightly. "I can't do it for you. It's always been something you need to work on for yourself."

He understood that she'd had to be alone? Maybe not that she'd needed two years. But still, he'd always been waiting. Aware it was only them...

Looking for the time they'd be able to get back together.

"I love you, Julio." Her voice was a scratchy mess.

His lips curled up, just slightly. As if he had a secret

no one else knew. "You know, when I first fell for you, I told you. My feelings might have grown as we did since that day you waded in to rescue Bristol from those bullies. But it's never quit. I've never stopped being in love with you."

He leaned in and touched his lips to hers.

Samantha settled into his touch. Not quite the same as before. It was different now, and she felt the sliver of grief between them over what they'd lost. Not just time but a life. One they would have raised together.

A little of her grief eased, knowing he understood. That he felt the same way.

Samantha held on tighter.

A thump made her flinch. Julio leaned back.

To their right, a section of drywall lifted. Slowly. So slowly. As if it weighed more than she'd have been able to move. And a face came into view, firefighter uniform and helmet. "Cap?" It was a female firefighter. "You good?"

"We're good. Get us out of here."

"Hold on. Got to get the wall braced so it doesn't come down on you." She disappeared out of sight.

Samantha wanted to move toward the hole and climb out of the opening.

"Wait," Julio said. "Until the timing is right."

She glanced at him. Wasn't that what they'd been doing all these years?

What was a few more minutes going to cost them?

TWENTY-SIX

The nurse helped slip the sling over Julio's head, securing his arm to his front. Pretty soon the pain meds they'd given him while they reset his dislocated shoulder would wear off. Until then, he could move slowly if he focused. Who knew how he'd feel when the truth of the pain he was in came to light.

"Thanks."

"Sure thing, hon." She gathered up her things. "I'll get your paperwork, and you can get out of here."

He was going to head right to Samantha's room as soon as he could. Through the glass of the door and the wall around it, he could see across the hall. The emergency department of the hospital in Benson had all glass-fronted rooms, so staff could see in if they needed to.

It meant he saw the fire chief, Greyson Frayer, step into view and speak with a different nurse than the one he'd been treated by.

Inevitably, Julio's thoughts slipped back to Samantha and the conversation they'd had. Not so much an end-of-life confessional, but pretty close to it. Each knew how the other felt. He'd stated his case as much as he could. Put all his cards on the table.

Taking her to his house—the place that was supposed to have been theirs—would either seal the deal or put an end to the whole thing. Which was probably why he hadn't invited her over yet. Though, he was pretty sure he would soon enough.

As soon as they'd been pulled from the burning wreckage of the firehouse, they'd been separated. Put on different ambulances. Treated and rushed to the hospital. He wanted to get on his knees and thank God no one else had been inside the building when it blew.

Though, he needed to figure out the implications of other possible scenarios.

Julio had no idea where his phone ended up. Samantha's had been shattered, but she'd used it for a flashlight. Even after her sister had replaced the screen after it was smashed when she was nearly strangled to death by Walter Barnes. He needed to message his parents and let them know he was all right, assuming they'd heard something happened to him. The need to connect was probably a result of nearly dying, realizing the frailty of his own mortality.

Live or die, he wanted it to be together with Samantha. He didn't want to think what would have happened if he'd lost her. Which he very well could have. Or she could have lost him.

They could've both died today.

Greyson knocked on the door, dressed in his chief uniform, minus whatever jacket he'd been wearing at the scene. Though his face and hands looked clean, ash had smudged his shirt front between two buttons, and his neck and hair were slick with a layer of grime.

Julio lifted his chin, and the chief came in. "Hey."

"Feeling okay?" Greyson looked him over.

"Better than I might've been if we'd been anywhere else." Another thing to ponder.

"Good. Ready for a rundown?"

Julio nodded.

"Two explosive devices at either end of the firehouse, so he was going for maximum destruction. One of them malfunctioned somehow. The resulting explosion wasn't as bad as it could've been. Wallace from your team is going through it. That was his initial assessment."

"Good. I trust Wallace." His colleague on the bomb squad was an officer in Benson PD and a former explosives expert in the army. "I wanna get in there. Take a look at the scene."

"I figured you probably would. But not before tomorrow. The whole place needs to be secure and cleaned up, and everything needs time to cool."

Julio pressed his lips together.

"You're okay. So is Detective Jesse," Greyson said. "I saw her on my way over. She's two rooms down with another woman and Detective Alvarez. They were talking."

"Thanks." Julio ran his available hand over his face. "Explosives?"

"It's a deviation," Greyson said. "All these fires, and elaborate scenes where he's blocking HVAC and trapping people. Now this?" He sighed out all the weight of being a chief that he carried every day, made worse by the fact they still didn't have a suspect.

"What about the school? Was *that* typical?" Julio turned so his feet hung off the side of the bed. He needed clean clothes—and shoes.

"Actually no. More like smoke bombs, according to your guy."

"Samantha said the kids were hiding in closets, like a lockdown drill."

Greyson nodded. "Vents were stopped up, so the smoke had nowhere to go. Heat cranked up, so it felt like there was a fire blazing somewhere in there. But no actual flames. Though, at the rate everything was going, something would've caught eventually. Electrical. Mechanical. There would've been a blaze, albeit pretty small at first."

Things always escalated if left alone. Everyone in the department knew to check and double-check elements of a scene to make sure all potential flares were taken care of. Anything ignored had the ability to come back to life in a second on its own.

Fire was like nothing else. It had a life of its own.

It acted. It reacted. It found a path and consumed fuel reaching for more. Like it was alive...and hungry.

"Did Wallace take a look?"

"He left the school after the firehouse blew," Greyson said. "I'm sure he's planning to go back when he's done."

Julio didn't envy the guy how many hours of overtime he would put in over the next couple of days. "He should forward everything to the taskforce admin so we can get the reports. Start putting them up against the profile the FBI has come up with. See if we can get a suspect list going."

"That's part of why I came." After a second pause, Greyson continued, "He hit us good. That school scene created chaos. Everyone was there. No one left in the house. Until you and Samantha went there."

"What are you saying?" Julio had his own ideas, but he needed someone else to state them aloud so he'd know he wasn't reaching.

"He lashed out at us. Created a scenario where he'd get maximum damage but little loss of life. None, in fact. But my guess is, he wouldn't have minded if you and Detective Jesse had been killed."

Julio nodded. "He tried to kill us on purpose."

"Maybe. Depending on when he stashed the explosives. They could've been waiting there for any amount of time, and he hits a button, or makes a call, and they go off right when he wants." Greyson folded his arms across his chest. "But he also crippled the fire department. He took out our house."

"Now, we'll be scrambling to house personnel and trucks until it's rebuilt."

"He knows us," Greyson said. "He knows the firehouse we moved from, the relic over on Marsten Street is a museum now. Too far to operate out of. We need to start praying now that no one gets killed because we took too long to respond. Because for the next few *months*, response times are gonna be longer than anyone likes."

"The implications might be something our arsonist isn't even aware of. Maybe this was purely personal, and he'll realize later he's put even more lives in jeopardy." Julio scratched his jaw, feeling the tension in his shoulder as he moved. Not good. He was going to be in pain for a *while*. But he and Samantha were alive.

The chief studied him. "What are you thinking?"

"This guy is nothing like your average pyromaniac. He might even not have that psychosis."

"But he likes to set fires."

"Seems to me like it's far more strategic than that." Julio thought for a moment. "He retraces Sylvana's history, killing people connected to his case. Now, he's evolved beyond that, and he's messing with our attempts to stop him."

But he didn't know where the attack on Samantha came into it.

"Explosives? That's a different tactic." Julio paused. "This guy has a plan."

"Any idea what it is?" Greyson asked.

"No, but I get the feeling this is nowhere near over."

Targeting him and Samantha might be a deviation, but it also might not. Julio had a feeling they were connected to it. Whether they liked it or not.

But it didn't matter. They were on the taskforce, which meant neither of them would rest until they had this guy in cuffs—or he was dead.

Then again, what if this was happening to them *because* they were on the taskforce?

It certainly felt personal. But no one else had been targeted, just them.

So what was it about him and Samantha that had set this guy off?

The door to his room opened again, and Captain Tennet stepped in.

Julio said, "Dominic." The guy might be over the task-force, but they were the same rank.

Tennet nodded. To Greyson he said, "Chief."

"Captain." Greyson nodded back. "What have you got for us?"

The difference between the two men caught Julio's

attention. The stark contrast between the two uniformed, clean-shaven men.

Greyson had been at the scene, getting dirty with the firefighters. Doing his job in a way that would always be hands on—not just because he'd been a firefighter on truck. Until Greyson had been caught in a deadly fire and burned in ways that confined him to desk duty.

Dominic Tennet had worked out of the office his entire career. He pushed paperwork, learned from books and conferences, and rarely got his hands dirty. But to his credit, Tennet had a keen mind for figuring out arson cases.

"Anything new?" Julio asked, determined to keep the peace until this guy was caught. They might have different ideas of what worked as far as tactics for flushing the guy out, but considering Julio had almost died today, and nearly lost Samantha, he was willing to seek out all the advice he could get.

"I'm afraid I need to confess something." Tennet cleared his throat, all his attention on Julio.

Greyson looked at Julio, then at the other captain.

"What's that?" Julio asked.

"I haven't been entirely forthcoming about what I know." Tennet frowned, his dark brows drawing together. Silver threaded through the dark hair on his temples. "I believe I might know who our arsonist is."

Julio flinched. "You do?" Keeping that knowledge to himself could've cost lives.

"I've researched a lot of arsonists in my career, attending classes on their development. Even teaching a few myself." The other captain seemed so proud of himself.

Julio would rather be wearing turnout gear, a tank

and mask, heading into a burning building. But he had to admit, he could see the appeal of learning and sharing knowledge. A different way of saving lives.

Tennet continued, "When Richard Sylvana's name came up in my research, I went to see him. More than once, actually. To try and figure out what encouraged him to do what he did."

"And you think you know who was interested enough to want to follow in his footsteps?"

Tennet nodded.

Greyson just stood stoic, his arms still folded. Absorbing the information before he figured out what to do with it.

"He told me that at one of the fires, he met a child," Tennet replied. "In fact, it was the last fire where he was arrested. As he was setting the devices, he found a little boy hiding in the laundry room. He told the child to run back to his room, and never thought of him again. He said the little boy told him that his name was Custard."

Julio frowned. "That's got to be a nickname."

Greyson nodded. "Have you ever found him?"

"I did some research into the fire, but never could figure out who the child was."

Julio said, "What makes you believe he's our arsonist now?"

Tennet shifted his stance, and as he did Julio spied a cross necklace under his shirt. He hadn't realized this guy was religious, but in a case like this one, it could be an asset.

And his knowledge of Sylvana could be key to unlocking the entire case. So long as Tennet didn't jump the gun with a press conference as he had before.

"Just a hunch," Tennet said. "Seems like whoever is

working now is connected to Sylvana, the original one, and it could very well be someone like this child. Richard actually told me the boy visited him. Years later. He'd turned into a fan."

Greyson unfolded his arms. "We need to figure out who this kid is and see if he fits the profile."

Julio nodded. "Before it's too late."

TWENTY-SEVEN

A few feet from the line for security at the tiny airport to the west of Benson, Samantha hugged her sister tight. No matter that it wasn't even six in the morning. The quicker she could get Bristol out of Dodge, the better.

It wasn't like she would be asleep if she'd been at home.

She'd tried to rest last night and wound up barely dozing, interspersed with fitful dreams about dark enclosed spaces. Some of the times Julio had been with her—usually dead, leaving her alone with his battered body. Other times, some faceless shadow followed her.

She'd caught herself before waking up screaming. But still, her throat was raw.

Samantha leaned back as Bristol patted her shoulder. She signed, *I'll be okay* and gave her another hug just because.

Then Bristol tipped her head to the side. Samantha pressed her lips together. A few feet away, Romeo looked at his shoes, then back up. Right. Of course.

Samantha nodded, signing, *I get the message.*

She walked away, giving the two of them a moment to say goodbye to each other. To her credit, Bristol had barely argued when Romeo and Samantha stated their case. With things heating up, and the arsonist growing bolder, neither of them wanted Bristol around. Not because her deafness made her more vulnerable, though it did. It just wasn't about that—it was about the fact they cared about her.

Samantha would have made the case whether her sister was a hearing person, or not, and with Romeo backing her up, Bristol hadn't had good reason to turn down a trip to stay with their parents in Phoenix for a few days.

Just until they found this guy.

She checked her phone, but there were no new messages. Julio must still be sleeping. They'd planned to meet at the morning briefing, but Samantha wanted to head to the prison and see if they could talk to Richard Sylvana, since they were over on this side of town anyway.

Samantha quit resisting temptation and glanced over at her sister and her partner. Arms wrapped around each other. Lips locked.

She turned away, rolling her eyes. It had only been days. *Days!* Geez, Romeo moved fast.

"Jesse!"

Samantha glanced over again at Romeo's call. Her sister, red cheeks and a flushed face, waved at her. Samantha signed *love you* and waved goodbye. Her sister did the same and headed for the security line.

Romeo gave her a single glance, then headed for Samantha. "She'll be good, right? By herself?"

She eyed her partner. "She's flown plenty of times by herself. She'll be fine."

Romeo didn't seem convinced.

"Let's go." She told him her idea about swinging by the prison and talking to Sylvana.

"About this custard kid thing?"

She'd briefed him when he woke up. On the couch in her apartment, where he'd spent the night. Making sure they were safe. Julio had filled her in via text late last night. They'd seen each other briefly at the hospital. It hadn't made sense to leave together when Romeo needed to take her and Bristol to their place, and he lived in the other direction. Greyson had given him a ride.

She and Julio had chatted over text for a while. Easier than talking aloud on the phone when she had more smoke inhalation to add to what she already had, and a million scrapes and bruises from being blown up.

Again.

With their conversation rolling through her mind, she felt like she'd need a million hours to process it all. She'd asked Bristol what she thought about Julio insisting she needed to figure things out on her own. That she needed to let go of the hurt and pain she'd been carrying, which her sister thought she'd hung on to because she needed to nurse the pain to keep from getting hurt again.

If she was damaged, she had an excuse to keep her broken heart to herself.

Bristol had told her to give the pain to God. To let Him take it away, rather than continue to allow it to hold her captive. But she'd also said that giving it up would leave a void, which she needed to then fill with hope and peace she could only find in God.

Her sister was turning into a minister. Samantha

hoped Romeo was ready for that in his life—and that his presence in her sister's world didn't mean her sister lost some of the vibrant faith she had.

In the end it was no surprise her sister had agreed with Julio, wanting her to make peace with God first. On her own. She needed faith not interconnected with her romantic relationship. She had to be solid on her own. For herself.

Bristol had always been number one in the Julio fan club. Okay, maybe number two. Now, she'd hung her star on someone else.

Speaking of...

Samantha slid into the car and buckled her seatbelt. When Romeo did the same, she said, "So that was pretty intense between you two."

She had no idea if it was their first kiss or not, but she watched the way Romeo reacted. The pull of a smile on his lips. The almost-shy way he said, "Bristol is amazing." He turned to her. "Guess I'm learning sign language. My mom already started, and Catalina—that's my sister, the one that's an SRO at the high school—she said she would, too."

"You already told your family about Bristol?"

He nodded, realizing what he'd indicated telling her that. "Yeah...Sorry. I know you didn't want me to meet her." He winced. "I can't help how I feel. She's amazing, and I guess it was the same for her. Like lightning."

Love at first sight.

"But if you think I should break it off," he continued, "'cause you think I'm not good enough for her—which I can be, I *will* be—I guess I can accept that."

And ruin what her sister had?

He was honest, at least, and it told Samantha how

much respect he had for her as his partner that he'd offered.

"That lightning?" Samantha said. "Julio says it was the same way for him. When he met me. Though, we were in middle school at the time."

"Then you know how it feels."

She nodded. "It's different with her, though?"

"I didn't believe I could feel this way about someone. I guess with all the other dates I've been on, women I was attracted to"—*you mean, a* lot *of women?*—"it's like I had no idea what real feelings were. Your sister just...line drive. Right out of the park. I'm mixing metaphors. But it's like one hit and you're in the stratosphere."

"If you hurt her in any way, I will kill you and make it look like you ran off after embezzling money from the department. In reality, you'll be buried in a shallow grave somewhere no one will ever find you. Probably multiple graves, because I will cut you into pieces."

Romeo stared at her.

"*If* you hurt her," she emphasized. "For the record, Julio will likely help me pull it off. The perfect crime."

He swallowed.

"Scared?"

He nodded.

"Good. Now drive."

Romeo gripped the wheel with both hands and drove to the prison.

"Thanks for driving, by the way." Samantha kept her voice light, aware of the effect her words had just had on him. Not completely pretending it had never happened but close. At least, now he knew where she stood. "I'm beat. I slept horribly, and I feel like I was hit by a bus."

"Just a building."

She smiled.

"Close your eyes. I'll wake you when we get there."

Samantha drifted for a while and woke when Romeo pulled into a space outside the prison. She drank a couple gulps of water from the bottle in the cup holder she was pretty sure was Bristol's and got out of the car to fix her hair. She tipped her head forward to gather up her hair, then secured it in a bun.

Romeo came around the car.

"Not a great solution, but I feel better at least." She figured she looked like she'd been hit by a building. "We should get coffee before the briefing."

"And you can take another nap on the way."

As they walked together to the front doors, he had a very brotherly look on his face, like he wanted to swing his arm around her shoulder the way Julio did with her sister. Guarding her. Keeping her safe in a comforting way.

Maybe it wouldn't be so bad to have him as her brother-in-law.

One day.

"I called while you were asleep," Romeo told her. "Warden Bernstein should be expecting us."

She must've been out to not have heard that or have been awakened by the conversation.

Sure enough, the warden was at the front desk when they got there. Standing behind it in a way that gave the impression his presence made the employees nervous. Like a demanding boss. He rounded the desk as they approached.

"Thank you for letting us in." Samantha shook his hand.

Bernstein winced. "Right. I'm afraid it may have been a wasted trip."

"Why's that?" Romeo asked.

Bernstein ushered them to a side room, off the main waiting area. He shut the door, closing the three of them in a quiet space not as cool as the entrance. He sat on the edge of a metal desk, some kind of maintenance office.

Probably not what the person who worked in here intended their office to be used for.

"When you said Detective Alvarez, I wasn't sure who you were coming to see. But when I saw you"—Bernstein motioned to Samantha—"I realized this was about Richard Sylvana. Right?"

Samantha nodded.

"I'm afraid you won't be able to talk to him. Sylvana was found dead in his cell earlier this morning. Looks like a heart attack, but I'm not sure if there will be an autopsy or not." Bernstein shrugged. "Sometimes families don't care enough to ask for one. Or the state won't pay for it if there's no sign of foul play."

"But they'll run a tox screen, right?" Romeo asked. "Make sure he wasn't poisoned?"

"They might not know what to test for specifically," Samantha said. "Something that wouldn't show up on the standard tests."

Romeo didn't look pleased.

She turned to the warden. "Did he share a cell?"

"Not last night," Bernstein said. "His cellmate has been in solitary the last week. He's due back tonight."

"Anyone come to see him recently who might've slipped him something? Or is there anyone in the inmate population you think might have reason to end his life?"

"All part of our investigation."

That was fair enough. Samantha didn't intend to step on his toes—or babysit a case not in her jurisdiction. Especially when it was unlikely their arsonist had come here and killed Sylvana. "Thank you for letting us know." She shook Bernstein's hand again. "We'll get out of your hair."

"Anytime." He led them to the door.

They headed back to the car. She called Julio and filled him in.

He let out a frustrated noise when she was done, which she agreed with. And it was better than letting loose a curse word—even if he wanted to.

Her phone buzzed against her ear. "Bristol is boarding her plane. Where are you now?"

"Walking to my car, outside my house. Quick breakfast with a buddy of mine from church, and then I'll be at the briefing."

She pictured him outside. In the open. She turned away from Romeo and managed to say, "Be careful. Stay safe."

"Sammy." He said her name in a soft voice. "I could get used to that again." Then he added, "I'll be all right."

She bit her lip. "See you soon."

TWENTY-EIGHT

Julio scanned the conference room in the FBI office off the side of the PD building. Looking for Samantha. She and Romeo should be here already —he was surprised she hadn't beaten him here.

Special Agent Addie Franklin smiled at him. "Good morning, Captain. Feeling better?" She might've been up in the night with her young child, but she certainly didn't show it.

"I'll feel better when we catch this guy."

"The detective isn't with you?" she asked.

"She and her partner took Samantha's sister to the airport. She decided to go on an impromptu trip to see their parents."

Addie nodded. "Wise choice. You didn't manage to persuade Samantha to go with her?"

"It didn't even occur to me to ask if she would." He frowned. Should he have? Maybe the dislocated shoulder was affecting his judgment. But who could blame a guy for that?

"Another wise choice, Captain." Addie saluted with

her coffee mug. "She's a police detective. She needs to do her job."

Julio didn't really know what to say to Addie about that. Though it seemed as if she thought she'd given him some sage advice.

In order to get coffee, he had to move out of someone's way, given he was in the aisle between the wall and the chair backs, which were pushed up against the table. He grabbed a mug, which was difficult given he was basically one-handed with his arm in a sling.

He'd been right about the pain. He'd awoken in the middle of the night, needing the pain meds the doctor had prescribed him. Julio would be on desk duty for a while, but no way was he giving up this case when this guy had tried to kill him and Samantha.

He took a seat.

Across the far end of the table, Special Agent Addie Franklin looked through the papers in front of her. A couple arson investigation and police admins sat to one side, down from a police lieutenant in uniform.

"We aren't all here, but we don't have time to waste." Addie glanced at the clock on the wall. "I believe we're missing Captain Tennet and our two Intelligence Division detectives. Is that all?"

The FD admin said, "Captain Tennet hasn't shown up to work yet this morning."

Julio frowned. It was past nine already. "Have you tried calling him?"

The older woman nodded. "He also isn't answering his phone. I spotted Sergeant Deerdan on my way in, and she said she'd send a couple of uniformed officers over to his house."

"Good idea," Julio said.

He figured everyone was wondering if the guy was their arsonist's latest victim. As much as he didn't exactly get along with the Dominic Tennet, he didn't wish ill of the guy.

He looked around. Flipped his phone over on the table. Still nothing from Samantha, and no sign of her. On the phone, she'd been worried about him being alone on the street. Enough she wanted to make sure he was protected.

He had checked behind him periodically on the drive over here, watching for a tail. But he hadn't seen anyone. Wherever their arsonist was today, he wasn't watching Julio.

Which made him wonder if the guy was watching Samantha.

"All right, then. Let's get started." Addie stood. "I've been comparing the profile I came up with to the incidents so far. At least what we can attribute to this guy." She glanced around. "A profile isn't a fact sheet. It's a living thing that grows and changes as we add information gleaned from his actions, and things like this manifesto." She tapped her index finger on one of the papers.

Julio figured all of it came together to paint a unique picture.

She continued, "Your ordinary pyromaniac wants to set as many fires as possible. It's a compulsion. A thrill, watching flames consume the fuel."

"If that was the case with this guy," Julio said, "we would have a lot more smaller fires and test fires on our hands."

"That's the thing." She glanced at him. "There are. But we had to go digging in the last five years of fire department reports looking for them."

"Arsons?" Julio said.

"Most were listed as accidental, or mechanical. Not arson or anything close to being intentional."

He frowned. That made sense why Tennet hadn't brought them to the taskforce's attention. The arson investigator hadn't ever investigated those fires. Even if he had, firefighters on scene often trampled key evidence. Or cleanup destroyed what remained of a time device or whatever had ignited to start the fire in the first place.

"We found them by searching specifically for records that mentioned issues with the HVAC or fires anything like what Richard Sylvana set."

"How many?" the FD admin asked.

"A dozen," Addie said.

"You think they were practice fires?"

She looked at him. "I think he's been working on this project a long time."

Julio swallowed too much hot coffee at once. He didn't like the idea of being a target. Where was Samantha? Maybe she was suffering the aftereffect of what had happened and needed help. Romeo had better be there if that was the case.

Addie continued, "The guy we're looking for is more than your average pyromaniac. He's highly intelligent. Strategic. He's a high-functioning sociopath, the kind of person who blends in enough you'll let down your guard. People aren't irrelevant to this guy. They aren't just too stupid to live if they get in the way of one of his fires. They are tools in his plan. Selected and then discarded."

The FD officer in the room looked up from making notes in his folder. "To what end?"

"He's a serial killer. One who knows enough about fire to pull this off. He's made it his specialty, in fact. Part of his psychosis. He considers himself unique among his peers. A step above."

The PD admin said, "Don't all serial murderers think that?"

"Yes," Addie said. "But this one has the knowledge base to pull it off."

Julio said, "That's terrifying."

"It should be." She looked at him, an impassive expression on her face. "Because he's focused on you right now."

Julio had been afraid of that.

"For starters, he had fire knowledge. He latched onto a method, following in Sylvana's footsteps. Next, he recreated the man's history."

"Too bad Sylvana is dead."

Everyone looked at the door, including Julio.

Romeo strode in holding a paper coffee cup in each hand. He came around the table and set the second one in front of Julio. Then took the seat beside him.

Where was Samantha?

Before he could ask, Romeo said, "We paid a visit to the prison. Richard Sylvana was found dead in his cell this morning. Cause unknown, but it didn't appear to be foul play."

Addie wrote something on her paper. "Thank you, Detective." Then she said, "First, the method. Then, religion drove him. Now, he's latched on to you and Detective Jesse." She pinned Julio with a stare.

"That's what I was afraid of." Julio figured anything they'd gathered so far could've been strategically planned in a way that was designed to throw them off.

He needed time to think it through, and people around him to do that with. In a way he couldn't do in a meeting like this. He needed to throw spaghetti at the wall, as it were. See what stuck.

Fine. Julio just wanted to work through it with Samantha.

Was anyone going to blame him for that?

"To what end?" Romeo said. "If my partner is still in danger, I need to know what I'm up against."

Addie tipped her head to the side, very slightly. "It'll be big. He wants recognition."

Another thing Julio was afraid of.

"I'll be looking for a complied list of possible suspects by the end of the day." She eyed Romeo. "We need to start somewhere and we can narrow it as we go."

"How do we avoid implicating anyone and everyone until we can get closer to the prime suspect?" Julio asked, tapping his coffee cup.

"Right now, anyone is a suspect. Even the people in this room." Addie lifted a file. "I have arson investigators going over the school and the firehouse. I'm sure you want to look at both, but there's another scene as well."

"Another fire?" Julio got up and rounded the table to grab the file from her.

Addie nodded. "Two days ago, a church across town burned down. It's not one of the mainstream congregations. They cater to more of a fringe crowd."

"Want me to interview the pastor?" Romeo offered.

"My thoughts exactly, Detective." Addie nodded. "I look forward to what you come up with. Report on my desk by lunch. Time is running out." She looked around the room. "This thing is heating up."

The meeting broke, and people started to disburse around the room.

Julio grabbed his paper cup of coffee and caught up to Romeo at the door. "Samantha?"

"She hung back to talk to Sergeant Deerdan," Romeo said. "Pretty sure the boss isn't so happy about Samantha being back at work today."

Julio winced. "Neither of us will be doing much." He figured he'd last until lunchtime at most, even just walking through fire scenes. But that was why they had a taskforce and it wasn't just him and Samantha working this case.

Romeo led him down the hall toward the rear of the building. "They were back here by the door. Deerdan was going out when we were coming in. I think she keeps tabs on our GPS."

Julio eyed a maintenance cart up against the wall. Wherever the maintenance person was, he couldn't see them.

"The guy was replacing tissue boxes and whatnot. Guess he's in the bathroom now." Romeo pushed through a heavy set of double doors.

The scent of motor oil and exhaust fumes hit Julio like a wave. The partially covered garage was open on three sides, and full of rows of black-and-white police vehicles, vans, and even a couple of golf carts. But no cops.

He looked around, but it was obvious Samantha wasn't out here.

Romeo strode down the middle of the motor pool, looking around.

The door behind Julio swung open, and a rotund male officer rushed out, breathless. "Why aren't the cameras working? What's going on?"

As if Julio had any idea.

Romeo said, "Over here!" and raced between vehicles. He ducked out of sight, then called out, "We need an ambulance!"

"I'll call for one." The officer rushed back inside.

Julio caught up to Romeo, skidding to a stop and slamming into the corner of an unmarked muscle car. Pain roiled through his shoulder, and he winced. But it wasn't Samantha lying on the ground.

Sergeant Deerdan gasped and started to sit.

"Easy." Romeo pushed back against her shoulder. "Don't try to move too much." He tugged off his jacket and pressed it against her abdomen, which was soaked with blood.

Julio crouched beside her. "Ambulance is on its way. What happened?"

Did this have something to do with the cameras being out?

Deerdan gasped. "He stabbed me and took her. Why didn't someone see?"

"Take it easy. Don't try to talk." Julio touched her shoulder.

The back doors opened. He stood in time to see two EMTs race through.

"Over here." Julio waved to them. "She's been stabbed." He crouched again.

Deerdan grabbed his arm with surprising strength. "You have to find her. He's gonna kill her."

"Who?" Julio had to shift out of the way of the medics.

Deerdan frowned. As if she thought he should already know. "He took her." Her eyes rolled back in her head as she passed out.

Romeo dragged him out of reach, now without his suit

jacket, which he'd used to put pressure on the wound. "Come on."

"Where?" Julio said. "Who took her? *Rome*, where is Samantha?"

Her partner's expression made Julio's heart squeeze in her chest.

"I have no idea."

TWENTY-NINE

Samantha scrambled backward, across wood beams. Irregular grain that dug into her palms. She reached the wall and sat up with her back to it. Breathing hard. Every ache and bruise she had decided to make itself known then.

She looked around, forcing her gaze from darting about to settling enough she could catalog the room around her. A cabin. Blinds and curtains on the couple windows pulled shut to create near darkness while the afternoon sun blazed down outside behind the covering of clouds.

The air was close, thick on this muggy day where the clouds hung low and the air seemed heavy with moisture—humid for here, not so humid compared to a lot of places. Soon enough, a weather system from the north would sweep down across the mountains, pushing out the Pacific heat. Bringing relief from the high temperatures and humidity.

Lightning strikes, probably thunder, too.

Maybe lightning would strike him while he was

outside. But then, she would be stuck in here where no one knew how to find her and she would die of starvation or some other thing before some hiker found her. Probably years from now.

Samantha heard the whimper escape her lips.

She forced out a choppy breath, carrying yet more of a sob with it.

She squeezed her eyes shut for the...however many times she'd done it. Thinking over what happened. Those few seconds when the unimaginable happened and she watched Deerdan...

Samantha sucked in another breath.

The maintenance guy, or so she'd thought. Now, she knew the curly hair had been a wig. The mustache was also stick on, along with a set of glasses with thick rims. Overalls and a nametag. He had to have had help because no one had questioned his entry into the police department. She could hardly believe it, but then who'd be expecting a wanted criminal to walk in the front door of their office?

Certainly not any cop she knew of.

Samantha took stock of herself in a disconnected sort of way—bending her feet, straightening and flexing her toes. Her hips were bruised but she could walk. He'd shoved her in here, making her walk all the way. At gunpoint.

She shuddered, and sweat rolled down her temples. She lifted her shoulder and wiped it against her hairline, which only made her think of Julio and his dislocated shoulder. She'd been on her way to the briefing, where she'd have seen him for the first time since they were loaded into separate ambulances.

They'd texted, but she'd wanted to get a look at him for herself.

Sergeant Deerdan had waylaid her and Romeo, talking about the case and how they'd sent her sister somewhere safe. When the conversation shifted to how she was doing, Romeo had excused himself. She and the sergeant had their personal conversation. Something she hadn't been expecting when she joined Intelligence, but she appreciated it nonetheless.

And then...

Her next breath caught in her throat.

Deerdan had shifted to move aside so the maintenance guy could get by them. He'd drawn a knife and slammed it into her stomach, pulling it out as fast as he'd shoved it in. She'd stiffened, shock on her face that probably mirrored the shock on Samantha's at watching it— but without the colossal pain of being stabbed in the abdomen by a six-inch blade in a police station.

Cameras.

Why had no one come running?

She could think it through now and conclude that none of it made sense. At the time, she'd barely had a second to think.

Even then, it wasn't enough.

He'd swung around, hit her with a stun gun, and she'd blacked out right around when he dumped her over his shoulder. There had been a white van, probably his, just inside the motor pool. Not many others around—because who would steal a car from the police? Security cameras, just in case.

Why had no one come running?

Okay, now she'd come full circle again. She was losing strength, and soon enough she would lose consciousness again. She could feel the fatigue creep at the edge of her awareness, snarling like a lion in a cage. Waiting to pounce.

She couldn't be out of it.

Samantha had no idea what he would do to her while she was unconscious.

Her mind could come up with all kinds of horrible scenarios, things she'd seen. Cases she'd worked. Gruesome deaths. People tortured and then murdered.

Her body flushed with cold, even though she was still sweating in the stifling heat.

A wide swath of sunlight blinded her as the front door to the cabin swung open, sending shards of glass into her head—at least, that was what the pain felt like. She winced against the impact. He slammed the door shut, rattling the whole cabin, but it bounced back a couple of inches and remained open.

She'd barely been able to make out the place in the bright light, but she had spotted a huge ancient refrigerator. Some furniture, but not much. He'd dumped her beside a bed. She reached out with her bound hands now and touched the ragged blanket on top of a bare mattress.

Samantha shuddered.

He walked toward her, a shadow in the darkness silhouetted by the strip of light where the door was still open a little. Her eyes still pulsed with flashes of light. He thought he was going to set the tone because he was in control.

So Samantha lifted her chin. Whether he could see her or not didn't matter. She needed to feel at least a smidgen in control of what was happening around her. "Hello, Walter."

She heard his low chuckle.

A disguise. A plan. "That was a risky move, going into the police station when you already assaulted an officer once."

"Didn't you hear? You started that fight. I was just defending myself."

"Is that what you told Marianne? That she started it."

In his mind, a guy like him could justify the fact beat he his wife and did who-knew-what to her. Unlike someone with no conscience, he believed he had every right to keep his wife in line—he thought he *had* to. And she should respect him and show it with every move she made.

Samantha pulled in her rambling thoughts. "I guess she deserved it."

"And so do you." He reached over and ran his finger down her cheek.

She bit the inside of her lip.

Could she get out the open door? She'd have to subdue him, but she was pretty sure she could run afterward. Assuming he didn't catch up to her and catch her again. After that, things would probably get worse.

"Did you kill Marianne?" Samantha said, keeping her voice steady. She had to ask—she needed to know what happened to the woman she'd been trying to help.

His low chuckle rumbled in front of her, far too close. She couldn't see his face, so maybe he couldn't see hers.

She looked around for something to use to subdue him. She had no gun, no shoes, and no watch. No badge, no backup, no phone or radio. No way out.

A glint on the floor caught her attention, a tiny flash of...something.

"You'll find out what happened to her."

When he did the same to Samantha? She needed a

different line of questioning, so she could use the time with him talking to figure a way out of this. So she said, "You went to a lot of trouble just to grab me. Maybe you should've killed me like you killed my sergeant. That's what you wanted to do on the street."

"A moment of weakness that won't happen again, I assure you."

So this was going to be cold and calculated? Great. "How did you get into the PD without anyone realizing who you were?"

"An arrangement. Not that I care what he wanted. It was a means to an end."

"What do you mean?"

He exhaled, which sounded a little like a chuckle. "A favor. He needed something taken in, I needed to take something out. An exchange, like the last time."

Someone wanted something taken *into* the PD. "Did you plant a device?" Was the police department going to explode? She had to warn someone!

"You think there was only one?" He wheezed, as though he thought that was so amusing.

"Who is he?" They'd thought it might be Walter at one point. "You applied to the fire department." Twelve years ago—that's what Tennet had told them. "You know him? Is he a firefighter?"

More laughter.

"You know who the arsonist is! Tell me!" She could barely think the desperation rang so loudly in her head. "Where did you meet him? Who is he?"

"You think this is an interrogation? I don't see why you need to know since there's nothing you can do about it before you die. He's all *nothing can stop my plan.* And, *it's God's will.*" Walter snorted. "Religious nut.

Warping his beliefs because he wants to burn it all down."

"Like a guy who beats his wife and believes it's justified?" Pride was Walter's religion.

His hand came out of nowhere. His open palm cracked across her cheek, forcing her head to the side while the pain blasted like a firework. Or a gunshot.

She squeezed her eyes shut, her face turned away from him.

Walter got up. She heard the clink of a chain. Before she even moved, he had it secured to the ties around her wrist.

She heard him walk away, and then the front door of the cabin shut.

Samantha tugged on the chain, the other end secured to the metal corner post of the bed, on the floor. Tears gathered in her eyes, spilling down her cheeks. The raw one stung. All she could think was...how many times had he chained Marianne on the floor by the bed?

This monster knew who the arsonist was.

He knew what their foe had planned. And if he went through with it, people at the police department could die. Maybe lots of them.

Samantha looked at the floor again, searching for the thing she'd seen. Why she fixated so hard on it right then, she wasn't sure. But then, she had no power here. No ability to save herself or the officers she worked with from dying. What she could do was hold herself together... while tears rolled down her face and her heart felt like it was breaking all over again.

How was she supposed to get out of this?

Her fingers found the slight difference, a raised bit between two wood planks. Ignoring a splinter that embedded itself in her finger, she pried out something tiny. She couldn't even see what it was.

The chain secured to her wrists clinked.

She lifted the tiny thing and found a chain attached to it—delicate like a necklace—that ran through her fingers. She held the now warm metal in the palm of one hand and moved her finger over it like she was reading braille.

A cross. On a chain, a necklace.

Marianne.

She'd been a believer.

Marianne had held out hope that God would save her. That she would be rescued from the situation she was in, even though Samantha had repeatedly asked her to testify against Walter.

She'd trusted God.

What had Marianne been thinking at the end? Had she kept her faith or fallen to despair? Sergeant Deerdan —dead as well because of Walter. Like Samantha would be soon enough.

Because God had abandoned them.

THIRTY

The sun was only an orange glow behind the high-rise across the street. Julio had lost count of how many coffees he'd had, but the table was littered with mugs and paper cups. Every few minutes another cop came in from the room-to-room search they'd conducted, or an FBI agent from downstairs showed up, adding to the mass of people in the room.

Someone hung up a phone. Lieutenant Gage Deluca, the former SWAT commander, called out across the room. "Deerdan is out of surgery."

More than one person whooped. Someone said, "Let's find this guy."

The door opened, and a dark-haired Hispanic woman wearing a blue police officer uniform came in. But Julio recognized her. He tapped Romeo on the shoulder. "Isn't that your sister?"

Romeo levered himself out of the office chair high up enough to say, "Cat!" Then he slumped back down while his sister weaved through people.

Across the room, a half dozen people stared at a map

on the wall, congregated around it as if that topographical map of Benson was the epicenter of the search for Samantha.

Cat squeezed his shoulder. "Simon is on his way over."

"Great," Romeo said. "Then everyone at Vanguard will be on the case."

"Isn't that a good thing?" Julio asked. "The more people we have looking for Samantha, the better. Right?"

A few feet away, some guy in a suit with a badge on his belt said, "A cop was nearly killed in our house. We don't need Vanguard's help."

Julio shut his mouth. They were all like this right now, determined to find the guy who'd tried to kill Sergeant Deerdan and had taken Samantha. Territorial. Embarrassed it had happened inside the police department. He didn't blame them, considering the fire department had been suckered into all being gone and left their house wide open to an attack that nearly killed Julio and Samantha.

They all wanted answers.

Considering Julio did as well, he wasn't arguing if they wanted to solve this themselves. They were letting the FBI help, at least.

"Here." Romeo called out to the room as a whole. "I've got him!"

Addie turned from the group by the map and shifted far enough Julio saw ears belonging to a German shepherd behind where she'd been standing. Former officer River Gaines stood by his search and rescue K-9, his wife, Tessa—nearby with her Belgian Malinois—affectionately called a Maligator. Probably his connection to the Benson

PD meant he'd been allowed into this inner circle nerve center.

Addie pointed to the wall. "Send it to the screen."

Romeo hit a few keys, and the huge TV on the wall flickered to a different window. A security feed of one of the halls. "This has to be outside of what was disabled."

Julio said, "He only turned off the cameras in the motor pool."

The officer who'd been on the motor pool desk, watching that area, several others, and signing vehicles in and out, must not have realized until it was too late.

Julio had wondered more than once if he'd still have a job tomorrow. But then, who'd have expected this? He'd been doing his job—not staring at the screen, watching cars and cops. The fact this attack had been so carefully coordinated told these cops—and Julio had agreed—that this was an elaborate plan. What Julio hadn't added was that only someone with inside information could have known enough to pull it off.

Walter Barnes didn't seem like he had that level of attention to detail. He was more of a "crime of opportunity" type of guy.

"There." Addie nodded. "You're right."

Lieutenant Deluca stared at the screen and frowned. "What is he doing? Is that a shoebox?"

Addie said, "He left it on that shelf."

The video footage showed a maintenance guy walking out of the room.

"Any other images of him?" Julio asked.

Someone at a laptop down from Romeo said, "I've got a shot of his face." She sent the image to the monitor on the wall.

Julio walked closer so he could get a better look.

"Who is that?"

"Run it through facial recognition. I want it checked against the DMV database first."

"Vanguard can do it faster."

He let all the conversation wash around him, the buzz of noise almost rippling against his ears. He still had a hard time with too much noise. Julio had grown up in an almost silent house, unless he played music on his personal CD player. His parents hadn't understood his need for a stereo given they couldn't hear most of the sound coming out. His dad could hear nothing, but his mom heard a kind of droning buzz when music played—or the TV. Enough to bother her, like a nearby fan irritated her ears in an almost painful way. They just weren't the kind of people who enjoyed music.

The TV screen froze. Someone grabbed the image with a mouse, cutting the face out and dragging a copy to another screen.

Julio reached up and stuck his fingers in his ears so he could focus on what he was seeing.

After a few seconds, someone touched his elbow. Addie. "Is everything okay?"

He lowered his hands and turned to her. "It's Walter Barnes."

The room silenced almost immediately.

She frowned. "This guy has a dark curly hair and a mustache." But she wasn't arguing with him—she was stating facts. "What makes you so sure it's him?"

She wanted to know why he was so certain. How he knew.

Apart from the fact that Julio had been up close and personal with him?

He turned to Addie. "Who interviewed him after he tried to kill Samantha?"

She looked at one of the cops—McCauley, now one of the PD chiefs. Julio hadn't noticed him come in. She repeated his question.

The captain frowned. "Sergeant Deerdan, I think."

Addie shifted her weight from one foot to the other. "So she's the only other person who got up close and personal with him."

"I'll pull up his booking photo." Romeo started typing.

She turned to Julio. "You're sure it's him?"

He could only nod. "It's his face."

She squeezed his shoulder.

Julio was about to explode out of his skin. What was Walter doing to her? Where had he taken her? Addie turned to one of her agents, the one with short hair who was married to a Benson detective. Hummet sat beside her, and on his other side was Lucas Westbrook. Both of them had shown up almost immediately.

Seemed like everyone was onboard with finding Samantha.

Figuring out who had stabbed Megan Deerdan.

Bringing him to justice.

These two, Special Agent...Julio was pretty sure it was Stella Davis—or Hummet if she used her married name—and Eric Hummet, had been there the day Samantha was blown out of that house with Romeo. Two years ago. The day she lost their baby.

Julio strode to the far side of the room and looked out the window.

Everyone had shown up. They would find her.

So why did he feel so useless?

"He's right," Detective Lucas Westbrook called out. "It's Walter Barnes."

Detective Hummet said, "It's just a first glance, but it's a match. The computers at Vanguard can confirm. And when we find him holding her captive, we'll have all the evidence we need to nail this guy to the wall."

Julio turned back to the blond man, Westbrook, and caught a look of respect sent his way—because he'd noticed it first?

Over the far side of the room, a younger guy came in. Long hair, down to his shoulders and civilian clothes. Not a cop. He spotted Cat, Romeo's sister, in the crowd and headed for her.

Another guy came in behind him who looked like Cat's guy, but a little bigger in the shoulders and arms. He held himself in the way a lot of cops did. This guy headed for Lucas, and their handshake shifted into a hug.

All these interconnected people.

He'd crossed paths with most of them in his career with the fire department. All these first responders, along with private citizens who pitched in. Police. FBI. Vanguard. The fire department did work that was a whole lot simpler, but still just as valuable in saving lives.

They were the ones who would save Samantha.

Julio looked at Addie. "Where is she?"

He needed to move. He needed a target, because he was itching to run. Like last time, when he'd raced over and launched himself at Walter Barnes before he could strangle Samantha.

Would Julio get there in time today?

Addie turned to the room. "I want all property listed in his name, or the name of any relatives. A former spouse, and her relatives. Give me all possibilities. He needs a place he can control. This is a guy with a domestic violence rap sheet who isn't afraid to take a shot at getting back at people who've wronged him."

"Is he the arsonist?" Deluca said.

Julio shook his head.

Addie said, "We have more circumstantial evidence that he isn't our guy than that he is." Not so conclusive, but she probably had to be careful not to say something definitive that was only a theory she couldn't prove.

"What's with the shoe boxes?" One of the officers pointed to the screen. "He left two more at other places inside the building."

Chief McCauley stood. "Let's go find out." He headed for the door, and half a dozen officers went with him.

Julio probably should follow, given he headed up the bomb squad, but he spotted a colleague from the PD who worked with him and let them go. They'd be fine—he had to believe that. He had to trust them because there was no way he was going to leave the search for Samantha.

"I've got something!"

Addie said, "What is it, Simon?"

The long-haired guy from Vanguard, Cat's guy, said, "Cabin up in the mountains. Belonged to his wife's father. She inherited it after his death, and it was signed over into her name with her maiden name as the surname."

"Walter didn't list himself on the deed?" Romeo scoffed. "Seems like something a wife beater would do." He sat back in his chair, looking collected, but under the table he bounced his knee.

The guy wanted to get out there and find his partner.

"We need to check it out," Julio said.

The search and rescue couple shifted. River Gaines,

the former officer, said, "Tessa and I can go for a walk in the woods. If he sees us coming, he'll just think we're hikers."

"Yeah," Gage Deluca said, "hikers with an armed response team as backup."

"Let's go check it out." Addie looked at Simon, and a couple of others. "I need the rest of you to hang back, see if you can find us alternates in case this thing turns out to be nothing."

Simon nodded. Cat slid into Romeo's seat.

"Come on, bro." Romeo tipped his head at the door. "Let's get you a vest."

Julio followed him to the door.

Lord, please let this be the place. Keep her safe—and alive—until we get there.

He could barely swallow past the lump in his throat, let alone voice the words aloud. God knew his heart. The Lord knew Julio wanted Samantha in his life for as long as he could have her there. That he would cherish her and protect her. If it was necessary, he would give his life to keep her safe.

It would mean they weren't together, but to him it would be worth it.

Otherwise, he would have to live without her—the guilt his only company. She would grieve him, sure. But the sense of failure plaguing him would be a thousand times worse.

How about neither of those?

Keep her safe, he repeated. *Don't let her lose faith in You.*

THIRTY-ONE

Sharp pain arced through her arm, and Samantha screamed—but no sound came out. Walter never loosened his grip on her wrist, squeezing so hard the bones felt like they were about to snap.

He drew the lit cigarette away from the tender skin on the inside of her arm. Tears rolled down her face. She'd screamed until her voice was raw, a shattered sound of what it should've been.

In that moment, she wasn't a sister, girlfriend, or friend. She wasn't a cop. A detective. An investigator. She was only one thing...

A victim.

She wanted to draw her legs up and kick him away—again—but it hadn't achieved anything last time, except to make Walter angry.

The door flung open so hard it hit the wall. Men poured in dressed in black, black helmets and huge rifles. All around Samantha washed in a wave of sound and movement.

Walter was dragged up, away from her.

She curled her legs up to her chest and made herself as small as possible in the space. The wash of commotion swam around her, cresting and falling like waves.

She spotted the letters SWAT on a vest, and a face she knew. Then another she recognized. Tears continued to streak down her face as Romeo crouched in front of her. "Let's get this off."

His hands touched her cheeks, reaching back to remove the gag from over her mouth. It slipped free, and she worked her jaw, wincing at the pain in her cheeks where it had split her lips and dug in.

"Let's get you out of here." He reached down to slide an arm under her knees.

Samantha smelled the sweat on him and flinched.

Romeo backed up. "Tell me what you need." But in his eyes, she saw he already knew.

Still, she lifted her bound hands and signed, *Coda.*

Romeo turned his head and called out, "Julio!" Then turned back to her and produced a knife.

Samantha held still while he wrestled her hands free. Then her feet. She sniffed.

"We need to get the medics in here," he said.

"No need." Julio swept in. "I've got it." He dumped a medical bag beside her and crouched. Looking at her with the dispassionate look of a trained EMT. Someone who went on call after call through a shift, no personal connection to any of them.

He dug around inside, hesitated, and then found what he was looking for.

And yet, there was a note of...something in him. She could see it at the edge of his expression. A tiny spark in his eyes that she probably wouldn't have noticed if she didn't know him so well. One that said he was barely hanging on.

He tugged on gloves, then took her hand. "Let me check you out, and then we'll go outside. Okay?"

The way he moved said his shoulder still hurt, but he wasn't wearing the sling. As though determined to ignore it.

Because of her.

Something switched in her. Like a lever that flipped. Samantha reached up with one hand and touched the side of his neck. It probably felt like she was hanging on for dear life, which is probably what she was doing—but she didn't want to think about how close to the edge she'd come.

She tugged his face close and pressed her lips to his. All of it was desperation, the need to be close, and the sheer relief of being alive.

He pulled back. "You're safe now."

Samantha stared into his eyes, feeling better than she had in hours. Better than she had since she'd been taken. She tried to speak but could only get out a squeak.

"We heard you. From outside." A crack appeared in his composure.

She signed, *Deerdan,* making it a question.

"She's out of surgery and stable," he said. "They repaired the damage, but it'll be a long road of healing."

She'd assumed that Deerdan was dead. That God hadn't shown up then, or with her in the cabin. No help. No hope. No way out. Now that Julio was here, she felt as if she had something to grasp. She'd never been someone who necessarily "felt" God with her. She'd sometimes thought that meant there was something wrong with her. As if God wasn't pleased.

Right now, she didn't have the mental strength to push everything aside and figure it out.

Julio touched something cold to the inside of her arm. "He got you good."

She bit her lip, more tears gathering in her eyes. Not because it hurt. Whatever Julio was doing made her arm feel better. She didn't want him to see the burns. And from the look on his face, he didn't like knowing what happened to her.

"Did he do anything else?"

Samantha stared at the emblem on his shirt.

"Sammy, did he touch you any other way?"

She managed to shake her head, and then had to sniff again.

"Bruises?"

She shrugged.

"Okay, think you can stand?" Julio wrapped her arm. "Or I can get a stretcher in here and we'll carry you."

She signed, *I want to walk.*

"Okay." He put his things in the medical bag and peeled off his gloves, a lot less tense than he'd been when he came in. He touched her cheek with his good hand, his palm warm against her face. "I'm glad you're okay. So glad. I was praying the whole time, asking God to intervene. To keep you safe. He did, and I'm so thankful."

She didn't have the voice to say that God hadn't shown up. She'd been rescued by cops and friends.

Julio shifted and helped her to her feet, sliding an arm across her back so he could take her weight and lead her to the door. Tucking her on his good side, so she wasn't against his injured shoulder.

The brightness outside glared, sending shards of pain

through her temples. She lifted a hand and shielded her eyes.

The shade over her face allowed her to see the ocean of people around the cabin.

So many cops. K-9 handlers, vests on with their dogs beside them. More cops. A few firefighters. They were walking back and forth up a narrow dirt road between the swaths of forest up a hill to this clearing.

Heat surrounded her, but the fresh breeze blowing through the trees was a much-needed change from inside the cabin. Her clothes clung to her.

As she picked her way across the clearing, tucked close to Julio, people started to notice. Cops turned. Watched. Someone clapped. Another guy said, "Good to see you, Jesse."

"Yeah, Detective. You held out." The man who'd said that raised a fist and pumped it in the air.

She bit the inside of her lip.

More turned, backing up until they had a clear path to go. A quarter mile down the road, a car backed up, stopping before they reached it, and Romeo jumped out. He ran around and opened the back door for her.

Samantha got close enough she could lift up and kiss his cheek.

"Hey, now."

She ignored Julio and signed, *Thank you.*

Romeo nodded. "Wish we could've got here sooner."

She figured they'd shown up right on time. Samantha put her hand on the top of the door and looked back at the ugly old cabin at the top of the hill. Not because she wanted to see it again before she left and never came here ever again. She wanted to look at the ocean of people.

All of whom had shown up here to get her back from Walter Barnes.

Deerdan was alive. Samantha's sister was safe. No one else had been hurt. Maybe God had shown up after all—not just in any way she'd realized. He'd kept worse things from happening to her than what she'd handled. Now that it was over, she was more than relieved, but she'd missed something.

God was real—she'd known that for years. The things He said were true.

It shouldn't be about what she could get out of it, or her faith was just about being selfish. And yet, what an abundance of things God had done today. She'd just had to see it for herself. As if she were still a young believer, looking for proof rather than having a testimony of things that were a solid foundation of knowledge. She'd be able to stand on that foundation, but it felt like she'd never taken the time to build it.

She'd *said* she was a Christian.

So why had she never acted like it? Or even truly believed Him in her heart, rather than just accepting it as logical and reasonable to do the right thing.

Now, she had proof. Like Walter in the back of a police car, being driven away. Arrested. And he wouldn't get out anytime soon since he'd attempted to murder a police sergeant and kidnapped another officer. She had a crowd of people who'd shown up. Brought together by God, because they cared about her or they were the kind of people who stepped up for a cop who'd been hurt. Didn't matter. It meant God could give her back Julio in her life.

"Hey." Julio tipped his face close to hers. "Ready to go?"

She didn't want to go to the hospital. She wanted to go home, but Bristol wasn't there. The place would be empty. She signed, *Your house.*

"You mean ours."

She stared at him.

Julio glanced at Romeo. "I'll give you an address. You can drop us off."

"Do I look like your driver?" Her partner sounded like he wanted to argue, but his tone was more like one he'd use with his sister, Cat, on the phone.

She signed, *Yes.* Julio chuckled.

They slid into the back seat, and Julio held her hand, one arm around her shoulders. She leaned over and put her head on his shoulder, closing her eyes. Feeling all the strength and warmth in him—the man God had made, just for her.

"You okay?" He touched her check. "That seemed like an important moment back there."

She asked God for the ability to speak, just a little. Her aching arms felt far too heavy to lift. Without either, she'd be unable to communicate at all, but even with that, she'd still be safe with these two men. The guy she'd always loved, and her partner and friend. She'd be able to get along just fine.

"You're exhausted, Sammy. Tell me later."

"I just realized how many gifts I've been given," she managed to whisper.

He nodded. Then he touched his lips to hers. "You should go to the hospital, but I also like the idea of you recuperating at my house."

She lifted her head and eyed him, one brow raised.

"I have a guest room."

Samantha laid her head on his shoulder again, able to

let go of the fear for just a second. Protected. Safe. There wasn't much of her life where she felt the way she did when she was with Julio. The man God had created just for her, and she knew he felt the same. There was never anyone else. There would never be anyone else.

She'd protected herself by cutting him out of her life.

But in the end, what kind of life had it been?

She moved her hand around so she could lace her fingers with his and hold on tight. Doing that reminded her she had done something similar when they were in high school. Samantha flexed her fingers so he loosened his. Then she drew her two middle fingers in, tucking them against his palm.

I love you.

Julio turned his head and kissed her temple, whispering, "Love you, too."

Samantha closed her eyes and pushed aside the pain long enough to let the fatigue claim her.

THIRTY-TWO

Julio felt when Samantha drifted off, and given what she'd been through, sleeping was the best thing for her now. Who knew what Walter had given her, or done to her, the things he'd put her through—even just mentally terrifying her.

The sick feeling sat like nausea in his gut.

Now that he had her back, all his emotions rushed in. Where he'd been pushing them aside and working the problem, now that she was safe in his arms, he could shake the fear he'd lost her for good.

Thank You. You kept her safe, and You will bind up her wounds. Help her to trust in You, more and more. Draw her close to You.

Julio rubbed his nose, which hurt his shoulder, but the pain was better than if they'd been too late to get her back. All he had was a dislocated shoulder that had been set to heal. She had a trail of cigarette burns on her arm, bumps and bruises all over. A mark on her cheek that looked like she'd been punched.

But she was okay. She would heal.

Julio's phone rang. He winced and tugged it from his pants pocket. No way to do it without it hurting, so he tried to keep as still and quiet as he could.

Samantha stirred anyway. She didn't need to go anywhere, though. Unless she wanted to.

He slid his thumb across the screen. Chief Greyson Frayer was calling. "Coda."

"We've got a problem."

"What's that?"

In the front seat, Romeo glanced in the rearview.

Greyson replied, "Reports of fire and small explosions all over the police department and at least three other buildings on the street."

"FD Headquarters?" Their building wasn't far from the police department, and city hall. What else had been targeted?

"Not yet. We're doing a room-by-room search."

"Those shoe boxes Walter was leaving all over the PD?" Julio's stomach knotted.

Romeo hit the gas and sped up, already on the highway that led back into Benson. Meanwhile, a huge crowd of officers were still up the hill, clearing the scene and collecting evidence that would nail Walter Barnes to the wall for what he'd done.

That meant, like the incident at the school, there weren't as many cops back at the house as there would be otherwise.

Samantha pushed off his leg and sat up. "Put it on speaker."

Her voice made him wince. She'd screamed herself hoarse. But he did as she requested. "Chief, what's going on?"

"Chief McCauley and his guys did a room-by-room search of the places Walter went," Greyson reported. "They counted four devices he left around the building. Things that would ignite on a timer and burn the box, then whatever it was around. Books. Files. A curtain. Each one was left up close and personal to a flammable material."

"But they removed them," Julio said.

"Apparently not enough of them." Greyson paused, and someone spoke in the background. "Get back here, Captain. We need everyone working now. Cops. Fire. EMS. Everyone. We're calling the Bureau of Land Management for the local wildland firefighters. This is big."

"Look." Romeo pointed out the front windshield, toward downtown Benson in the distance.

Samantha drew in a sharp breath.

"We have six buildings ablaze," Greyson said, "including the police department and fire department headquarters, and city hall."

Samantha covered her hand with her mouth.

Julio touched her knee. "Everyone is responding?"

"And we need all the help we can get. We missed devices. All of them...most of them."

Romeo said, "Walter needs to tell us who he is."

Greyson's response was, "Just as soon as we get these fires put out, you can ask him whatever questions you want. Probably in the park, because that'll be the only building still standing."

Just as soon as he said that, a clatter came across the phone line.

A matching boom in the distance made them all

flinch. Seconds later, a new plume of smoke rose into the sky.

"Chief?!"

"I'm good." Greyson gasped. "But Benson won't be if we don't get these fires put out. There are just too many of them. We don't have the personnel." He paused. "He had to have placed devices all over without us knowing."

"Then they weren't all placed by Walter," Julio said.

Romeo squeezed the steering wheel. "Maybe the arsonist got guys other than Walter in, wearing disguises. People who wanted to get back at the PD, or whoever else, with an axe to grind against them. Doing his dirty work so he could do this."

"We'll be there soon." Julio hung up the phone. "Drive faster, Rome."

Romeo flipped on his lights and sirens and hit the gas. He got them to Benson as fast as he could safely go, while the freeway going the other direction got steadily more crowded with people fleeing the city.

Julio prayed for all the first responders coming together to help people and try to save buildings. Everyone there would be occupied. A thought which gave him the ability to turn his mental attention to the arsonist who had done this.

Julio didn't want to wait until the police questioned Walter into giving up the name of the arsonist who paid him to deposit those shoe boxes. He didn't want to wait for them to find another person their suspect had paid to leave devices in another building.

The basic profile of a pyromaniac said he would be at the scene, watching things unfold. The need to see their handiwork was part of what drove them. That's why FD had long ago started recording the crowd at scenes. Firefighters were focused on their duties, trying to save lives and contain a blaze so there would be as little property damage as possible. They didn't spend time looking around at the crowd to see who was loitering.

If everyone today was focused on the fires—and the situation was overwhelming given the smoke rising from the street with all those buildings on it—no one would be looking around.

Julio was going to search for the guy.

If he could end it, here and now, that's what he was going to do.

"Get us as close as you can," Julio instructed.

Romeo turned onto the street and right into an ocean of people. Vehicles. Twilight was setting in, giving the whole place an orange glow. Firefighters raced around, water sprayed from multiple ladder trucks. He spotted a wildland truck, their hose all hooked up.

"There aren't going to be enough hydrants for this." Julio pushed open the door, overwhelmed by the scene on the street in front of him. The street blocked by vehicles, total chaos. Every ambulance in the county here or pulling onto the street.

People all over. Someone screaming across the street on the other side.

It was worse than the day a limo had exploded.

He scanned the roofs of buildings, looking for someone watching. Another high-rise, maybe a street over. Or behind him. Or at the far end, maybe.

There were a thousand places this guy could hide.

Flames licked out of open windows in the upper floors of the police department. Down the street, at city hall, black smoke chugged up into the sky from what had to be a hole in the roof.

Another building down from that, someone jumped off a roof. He raced to the sidewalk and caught a flash of air bags on the street. They'd cushioned the woman's fall with inflated mats. It had to be bad if the situation had reached that stage.

He turned back to the car, where Samantha still sat. He didn't like leaving her. They should've driven her somewhere nearby where she could wait safely, and maybe get some medical attention.

This situation...

He could hardly process the volume of fire on the street. Just one of these blazes would require multiple trucks to extinguish it.

This was a five alarm.

Maybe even worse than that. It would take everything they had to put it out.

Julio set his good hand on the roof of the car and leaned down to the open door. Before he could say anything, Samantha signed, *Go*.

He signed back, *Love you*. Still warm from when she'd signed that to him before, in the car. The way she had years ago. He couldn't believe he'd forgotten it.

Romeo had already run off.

Julio dug a radio out of the duffel on the front seat and handed her his phone.

She gave him a soft look, but she really did look exhausted.

The woman needed to stay put. And he could tell she wanted to fall asleep, so that worked.

Julio twisted the dial on the radio and let the chatter wash over him, quick snatches of conversation. He switched between channels and heard another firehouse doing the same. Someone had divided the response into sections, organizing it.

He went to a channel the bosses used. "This is Captain Coda. I'm going to look for the arsonist."

THIRTY-THREE

Samantha watched Julio walk away into a sea of chaos. She shuffled down in the seat and closed her eyes against the cacophony of noise and movement. Settling into the feeling she'd had with Julio and Romeo here, the security of being safeguarded.

Even with them gone, she felt it.

Maybe that was God's grace. His mercy. The peace she could feel even though she was alone. She might've been unable to feel Him in that cabin, but He had been there. Just because she didn't "feel" God's presence didn't mean He wasn't there.

"I trust You." She whispered the words, barely a sound emerging from her lips. "Thank You for saving me."

Julio's phone buzzed under her hand.

She flipped it over and saw a text from his parents, part of a group thread. She entered the code he'd always set for his phone PIN—the date of the day they'd met.

Once unlocked, the screen displayed the thread, friendly family chatter. The small talk of people who would be forever connected. Who knew to their souls they were cared for.

Samantha needed to use the video call feature, to make sure Bristol was all right.

She settled for a text.

> It's Sam. I'm good. We all are. But pray for Benson. Downtown is on fire.

The door beside her opened. Julio wouldn't be back yet, so instinct had her slip the phone out of sight under her leg. Someone leaned down. Captain Tennet—Dominic.

"Everything okay in here?" he asked.

She nodded, pointing to her throat and mouthing, *Can't speak.*

"You're too close to personnel and the fires. If you can walk, we should get you farther away from here." He backed up and waved her out of the car.

Samantha slid across the seat, which was more difficult than she'd have thought it would be. She tucked the phone in the back of her belt and flipped her shirt over it. Not foolproof, but there weren't many other places she could put it. Julio probably didn't have Romeo's number, so how would she be able to contact him if something happened?

Which was crazy. This guy was a fire department captain. Why would he do anything to her?

She climbed out of the car and looked around, as if to ask where they were going.

"This way." He touched her elbow. "There's a makeshift shelter in the bank building."

She thought that was quite close, given the building beside it was on fire, but she went with him. She might've had a rough day, but all in all, her injuries were minimal. And she thought that maybe—just maybe—there was enough energy in her to turn feral if the situation called for it.

Kind of like the day she'd faced down Bristol's bullies.

The day she'd met Julio.

He'd saved her from getting expelled for all the fights she'd landed in protecting her sister. And why not? Her parents had expected her to show up for Bristol as if she couldn't protect herself, or even speak for herself. Meanwhile, her sister had been bound and determined to throw off all constraints and make as many memories for herself as possible.

Tennet pulled open the door. "In here."

She managed to say, "You aren't helping with the fires?"

"I'm more of an office type. That's why I landed in investigation." He led her across a lobby, empty of anyone. This was supposed to be a shelter type place? Somewhere people holed up until the danger had passed.

"Where are we going?"

"Up to the second floor."

Yeah, no. "I think I should just head down the street. Go find somewhere to stay out of the way. In case the car isn't far enough."

His touch on her elbow turned to a grasp. She sucked in a breath as his grip turned punishing. She twisted around, nailing him in the diaphragm with the heel of her other hand.

He puffed out a breath, but didn't let go of her. His other hand produced a gun. "Not a good idea. After all, if you run, how are we going to watch Benson burn together?" He dragged her to the elevator and hit the UP button with a kick of his foot.

Samantha wanted to fight him, get away and run for it. The loaded gun pointed at her stalled her before she could even figure out how to subdue the bigger man so that she could make a run for it.

Then he would surely shoot her in the back.

He dragged her into the elevator.

"You aren't going to get away with this," Samantha warned. She just had to figure out how to request backup on Julio's phone, behind her back, with a gun in her face. "Someone will figure out what you did."

Dominic's face twisted into a grimace. "No one has ever known." He laughed. "It got too easy, setting fires. I needed a new challenge."

"Sylvana."

"Worth imitating, learning from." The elevator rose. "And then I surpassed him. I became greater than the master, and now I will complete my work and no one will mistake it for anything other than me. Doing what I was born to do."

"Destroy." She stared at him, her mind flinging around solutions like a pinball machine, unable to settle on one thing.

"Ascend."

And she was supposed to go with him?

The elevator stopped on the top floor. Doors slid open, and he shoved her into the hall.

Samantha slid the phone out because she had to try. She couldn't *not* try—or there would be no solution. No help. No backup.

Lord...

She didn't even know what to ask for. But God knew.

He would show up, in those small ways she'd been missing. Directing people. Bringing her family together—her brothers and sisters who bled blue. And the fire captain she'd loved since middle school. Her partner. People she'd never met but had heard stories about, and they'd shown up to find her.

As if she was worth showing up for.

She typed the pin code without looking. At the end of the hall, she looked down. Quick enough to see she'd unlocked the phone. Green button. *Call Romeo.* That wasn't going to work. Frayer was an option—she could call his chief.

Samantha lifted her gaze on where they were going and kept the phone out of sight. Maybe Dominic didn't care enough to see what she was doing, too fixated on his task. Whatever plan he had in place.

She stumbled on the carpet toward a fire door at the end, marked ROOF.

He nodded. "Through there."

At the same time she hit the handle, she looked down at the contacts list and saw ALVAREZ, R. Samantha hit the Call button and slid the phone down her front, praying it would remain in her hand out of sight. "Where are we going?"

There was no way they'd be able to hear her voice through the phone line.

But they might be able to hear Dominic's.

"Up." His voice echoed through the stairwell.

"Why do we need to be on the roof?"

"You'll see."

She reached the top of the stairwell.

"Faster now."

Samantha stumbled out into open air, filled with smoke. A plane flew overhead, followed by a helicopter carrying a water container. Probably a good idea to call in people who dealt with huge fires in a situation like this where she could barely breathe. Multiple buildings were ablaze.

The whole thing was overwhelming.

She wanted to lie down and curl up into a ball until it was over.

But at the same time, she had their suspect right behind her.

"The bank isn't affected by the fire." Samantha tried to speak loudly enough for whoever was on the line to hear. Had Romeo answered and not hung up? She had no idea. "What are we doing on the roof, Dominic?" They needed as much information as possible if they were going to rescue her and stop him.

"The bank isn't affected by fire...yet." Dominic grinned, as though pleased with himself, then shoved her out into the middle of the roof.

"What do you want?" she asked, her tone pitiful. "You're destroying Benson!"

"I will ascend. And you're coming with me." Dominic tipped his head back and laughed, his arms outstretched.

The building below them rumbled. The structure shuddered and shook beneath her feet. She scrambled back to the edge, stumbling to the ground and slamming against a low wall at the edge.

Lord Jesus, help me.

The expanse between her and Dominic dropped down into the floor below, and a cavern erupted under them as the building was consumed by flames. Only a ring around the opening remained. Flames licking up through the break where the floor had fallen away.

Dominic lifted his hands to the sky.

THIRTY-FOUR

Julio sprinted up the stairs. The whole building had rocked, but he refused to look down the stairs, where the concrete had fallen away in a wash of flames. He knew what that meant.

The arsonist had rigged this building but not ignited the devices with the others. He'd waited as part of his plan.

Lured Samantha to the roof.

But she'd managed to call her partner.

Thank You.

As soon as Romeo found him, saying she was on the phone talking to someone else, he'd grabbed all the gear he could find nearby and sprinted this way. Turned out all he had was a Pulaski from some wildland firefighter's gear. They'd probably be super mad when they discovered it was missing, but Julio would make sure they got their two-headed axe back.

Whether it had blood on it when he returned it was another story.

He pumped his legs, headed for the top floor. No

hand on the rail, just the axe in his good hand and the other tight to his side.

Dominic.

Julio was going to kill the guy for being the one behind this.

The building shuddered, including the wall to his left. He rounded a landing, and flames licked behind the glass window on the door.

Julio pressed on.

Right up to the top floor.

He'd given Romeo instructions but refused to allow the guy to come up here with him. It was far too dangerous for both of them to come.

Julio shoved open the door, and wind whipped his hair and face.

Dominic stood to the left, on one side of a chasm below throwing flames up into the sky. Samantha had huddled against the wall on the right. She looked terrified.

"Dominic!"

The arson captain swung around to him with his hands empty.

Good, because Julio didn't have a gun.

Dominic Tennet's mouth split into a wide smile that almost looked demonic. "I did it! And now you're here! We all die together. The beginning and the end."

"Stand down." Julio edged around the circle toward Samantha. "It's over, Dominic."

"This is the end!" As if he agreed with what Julio had said?

Julio kept taking small side steps around the circle. He assessed the building, and figured with Dominic's knowledge, the whole thing would collapse in on itself soon enough.

They might only have seconds.

"You didn't have to do this," Julio said. "You killed people."

"I purified them!"

Yeah, this guy was bananas crazy. How had he not seen it before? "You shouldn't have done this."

Julio wasn't going to let him kill anyone else. Definitely not him and Samantha when they'd only just found each other.

Dominic shifted closer to the edge.

Julio reached out a hand, and Samantha grabbed it.

She stood, levering herself up on his good arm, then pressed against his side. "How are we going to get down from here?" She knew he wasn't going to let her die. She didn't even consider it, because she knew he had a plan.

He wrapped his good arm around her waist. "We have to give them a minute to get into place."

"He had a gun. I don't know where it went." Her voice still sounded painful.

Time was running out.

"It doesn't have to end like this, Dom. You don't have to stay up here." Julio motioned with his free hand. "Come with us."

"No one is leaving!" Tennet screamed. "You aren't going anywhere!"

Julio tugged Samantha tighter against him and said quietly, "Trust me?"

She nodded. "Always."

He felt the gentle touch of her fingers on his abdomen, and his muscles flexed.

Across the expanse of the roof, a burst of flames shot up into the sky. Samantha tensed. Julio took a half step back.

Dominic said, "This ends, now!"

"Not for us."

The building shuddered.

Julio shifted Samantha another step back. "Get ready."

He heard the crackles begin. The heat in the center of the opening increased. Things were going to reach a fever pitch in seconds.

Dominic screamed, equal parts laughter and terror.

Julio spun Samantha to the edge and looked over.

"It's really far down," she said.

"We don't have a choice," he said. "The whole building is going to come down." He glanced over his shoulder in time to see a burst of flames collapse the floor under Dominic's feet.

The arsonist fell down, tumbling into the great pit of flames under him. At the same time, the building swayed. The floor beneath them began to crack.

Julio stepped on the edge, holding tight to Samantha. "I love you."

"Just do it." She tucked in close to him, her arms around his neck.

Julio let them fall first, rather than stepping off the ledge. He needed them to fall horizontally not vertically.

Samantha screamed.

Wind battered their clothes.

He looked over her shoulder enough to know his aim had been spot on.

A second later, they slammed into the inflated canvas the firefighters had set up. They hit the bottom and bounced up, nearly launched off the side. Hands caught them, dragging the two of them to the ground.

Samantha flushed, grasping hands to stay upright.

Julio let one of the engine guys help him stand, then he slid his arms around her waist and tugged her close.

They were alive.

Julio lowered his mouth to hers, sweeping her up toward him at the same time. He heard a hoarse laugh, and she touched his cheeks, then her arms snaked around the back of his neck.

Someone whooped.

Julio found a slice of joy in the middle of chaos. Peace and life, hope and love—all of it there even in the midst of darkness and pain. The way it was always destined to be.

Because God had always meant them for each other.

He lifted his head and looked around. There was still so much work to do. Cleanup. Disaster recovery.

"Someone find me the chaplain!" he yelled.

Hmm. Unless Samantha wanted to wait for her sister to get back in town. Yeah, she probably did. "Actually…"

"No, I like this idea." She smiled. "If I can speak, I'll say 'I do' to you anytime."

Julio grinned. "Sure?"

"We can have a reception later. Make a fuss."

Julio whooped. "We're getting married!"

EPILOGUE

Two days later

Samantha pulled the car over to a lot designated for first responders helping with the cleanup. The police department, fire department, and city hall had been decimated. Most of the buildings on the street would have to be pulled down and completely rebuilt.

At the last count, twelve people had lost their lives—including the man responsible, Dominic Tennet. A career arson investigator who'd been hiding a dark and dangerous secret for decades. In the coming weeks, no doubt additional cases would be pulled out of the proverbial file cabinets, attributed to him, and then marked closed.

She parked the car and tugged both paper cups of coffee from the cupholders before making her way to where Julio should be.

In the command center, where cleanup efforts were

being coordinated from. A series of white canvas tents with the sides rolled up. White folding tables. Clipboards. Two staffers from city hall in office attire, completely out of place in the dust and debris of what was left of the street.

He stood to one side, looking over a table and something spread over the surface—building blueprints. Around him stood four firefighters, their uniforms slightly different than the Benson guys. Each one had RESCUE written across the shoulders of their turnout coats, as well as a name along the bottom hem.

The closest one was CRAWFORD. The other names were FOSTER, RICE, and STEPHENS.

"Coda?" She had told him she was bringing coffee. He'd had an early meeting, and no one wanted to see her for at least a week. Though, she still had a report to write.

The firefighters all turned to her, and she handed Julio his coffee.

"Guys." He squeezed between them and came over to put his arm around her. The coffee ended up on her shoulder. "This is her. My wife." He sounded so proud of her—of them—and the rash decision they'd made to not waste a single moment more.

"Samantha." She'd nearly said, "Jesse" but caught herself. Though, she planned to keep her maiden name for work purposes, given it was easier to say than Espinoza-Vasquez.

The first guy stuck his hand out. "Byrce Crawford. I'm the lieutenant." He had brown hair, slightly damp from sweat, and a swipe of ash on his cheek.

"They're from Last Chance County," Julio said. "Rescue Squad."

"These are my guys." Bryce Crawford motioned to

each one in turn. "Eddie Rice." Young, and African American. Movie star handsome.

"Zach Stephens." Also young, and with kind dark eyes. A little smaller than the others, but she figured he was scrappy when he needed to be.

"And Ridge Foster." Darker hair, classically handsome. But with an edge Samantha wasn't sure about. He could play that boy-next-door look, but there was more to this guy. "We've had some personnel changes recently, so we're getting our training time in as a new squad."

Foster lifted his chin. "Nice to meet you."

Julio said, "They came over to help with the cleanup, since we're shorthanded."

"Wow, guys, I know everyone appreciates it." She smiled at them all.

"Especially when I can't do nothin' with this arm."

Her injuries weren't something she was going to talk about. She'd worn a long-sleeved shirt to cover the bandages on her arms, despite the heat. The only thing that helped was working alongside Julio during the day—and then going home with him at night. Wearing a ring on her finger that he'd slid on there in front of the chaplain who'd married them. The same way she'd slid the gold band on his ring finger.

"We've got you covered." Crawford slapped his gloves on his hand. "We'll get to work."

"But...one thing..." The one named Foster seemed hesitant.

"What's up?" Julio said.

"We work with a firefighter that I believe used to work out of Benson FD. Not that she talks much about you guys. I just wondered if you knew her." Foster paused. "Amelia Patterson."

Julio grunted. "She's in Last Chance County?"

The guys all frowned. Zack looked at his lieutenant like a kid brother at his older sibling.

Foster studied Julio. "So you worked with her?"

"That was a bad house. I took over as captain a couple of years ago. Half the squads stationed there went at the same time the captain got canned. Not sure what happened to him after he was fired, though. Probably should've gone to prison." Julio took a deep breath. "Let's just say, if she's in Last Chance County with you guys, then she's in a better spot than she ever was here."

They filed out.

Samantha said, "Any idea what that was about?"

Julio watched them go, then shook his head. "We had a captain who should never have been promoted to that position. One of those kinds of cancers in the organization who spread their poison so far it takes years to grasp the full effect."

"I'm glad this Amelia person got out, then."

He nodded. "Me, too. Fresh starts are good for everyone."

"And second chances." She smiled up at him. Her husband. "Those are my favorite."

He kissed her but didn't linger. There were people around and plenty of work to do coordinating cleanup.

"Bristol called me. She's kinda mad, but only because Romeo got to be a witness and she didn't. But I promised her we'd do the whole vow renewal, white dress, maid of honor thing as soon as we get the chance. Have a big party and invite everyone we know, even the people we don't like—just so we can rub it in their faces."

Julio chuckled. "I like your style."

"I already knew that."

He shifted his hold on her and held up the paper coffee cup. "To forever."

"I'll drink to that." She tapped her cup against his. "Forever."

They sipped their coffee.

He sighed. "Guess we should get back to work."

"It never ends."

KEEP READING FOR...

• Where to find more great Lisa Phillips books.

• How to sign up for Lisa's newsletter and get a FREE book.

• Where to find Lisa on social media.

ABOUT THE AUTHOR

Find out more about Lisa Phillips at her website, where you'll discover more romantic suspense fan-favorite series and heart-pounding thriller novels.
https://authorlisaphillips.com/about/

If you loved this book, please consider sharing about it on social media. Or leave a review at your book retailer website, on Goodreads, or on Bookbub. Your review will help others find great books to entertain and encourage them!

Signup for Lisa's newsletter by scanning the QR code below to stay updated on sales, new releases, and recommendations for your TBR pile. New Subscribers even get a FREE book!

Find Lisa on Social Media!

facebook.com/authorlisaphillips

instagram.com/lisaphillipsbks

bookbub.com/authors/lisa-phillips

Find out more about Benson First Responders on the series page:

https://authorlisaphillips.com/product-tag/benson-first-responders/

Benson First Responders is a continuation of Last Chance Downrange. Read the whole Last Chance Downrange series now!

Point of Impact

Hard Target

Hollow Point

Terminal Velocity

Audio Available from Podium Publishing

Find more stories based in Last Chance County at:

https://authorlisaphillips.com/product-tag/last-chance-county/

Other series by Lisa:

Brand of Justice (Thriller series)

Benson First Responders (Christian Romantic Suspense)

Last Chance Fire & Rescue (Sunrise Publishing)

Chevalier Protection Specialists

Last Chance County

Northwest Counter-Terrorism Taskforce

Double Down

WITSEC Town (Sanctuary)

And numerous other titles including several from

Love Inspired Suspense.

Find the complete list here:

https://authorlisaphillips.com/all-books/

9 798888 552252 6